WESTERN WP PROMISES

The Texan's Secret

LINDA WARREN

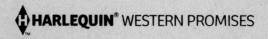

HARLEQUIN® WESTERN PROMISES

Recycling programs
for this product may
not exist in your area.

ISBN-13: 978-0-373-00341-9

The Texan's Secret

Printed in U.S.A.

WESTERN WP PROMISES

SHIPMENT 5

Rodeo Daddy by Marin Thomas
His Medicine Woman by Stella Bagwell
A Real Live Cowboy by Judy Duarte
Wyatt's Ready-Made Family by Patricia Thayer
The Cowboy Code by Christine Wenger
A Rancher's Pride by Barbara White Daille

SHIPMENT 6

Cowboy Be Mine by Tina Leonard
Big Sky Bride, Be Mine! by Victoria Pade
Hard Case Cowboy by Nina Bruhns
Texas Heir by Linda Warren
Bachelor Cowboy by Roxann Delaney
The Forgotten Cowboy by Kara Lennox
The Prodigal Texan by Lynnette Kent

SHIPMENT 7

The Bull Rider's Secret by Marin Thomas
Lone Star Daddy by Stella Bagwell
The Cowboy and the Princess by Myrna Mackenzie
Dylan's Last Dare by Patricia Thayer
Made for a Texas Marriage by Crystal Green
Cinderella and the Cowboy by Judy Christenberry

SHIPMENT 8

Samantha's Cowboy by Marin Thomas
Cowboy at the Crossroads by Linda Warren
Rancher and Protector by Judy Christenberry
Texas Trouble by Kathleen O'Brien
Vegas Two-Step by Liz Talley
A Cowgirl's Secret by Laura Marie Altom

Two-time RITA® Award–nominated and award-winning author **Linda Warren** loves her job, writing happily-ever-after books for Harlequin. Drawing upon her years of growing up on a farm/ranch in Texas, she writes with an emotional punch about sexy heroes, feisty heroines and broken families, all set against the backdrop of Texas. Her favorite pastime is sitting on her patio with her husband watching the wildlife. Learn more about Linda and her books at her website, lindawarren.net, or on Facebook, LindaWarrenAuthor, or follow @texauthor on Twitter.

Books by Linda Warren

Harlequin American Romance

The Christmas Cradle
Christmas, Texas Style
"Merry Texmas"
The Cowboy's Return
Once a Cowboy
Texas Heir
The Sheriff of Horseshoe, Texas
Her Christmas Hero
Tomas: Cowboy Homecoming
One Night in Texas
A Texas Holiday Miracle

Texas Rebels
Texas Rebels: Egan
Texas Rebels: Falcon

I dedicate this book to my patient editor,
Kathleen Scheibling, who stuck with me
during a really rough time.
Thank you!

And to Paula Eykelhof, for just caring.

And to the special angels who were there when
they didn't have to be:
Diannia, Sondra and LaVal.

And, as always, to my hero, Sonny.

Acknowledgments
A special thanks to:

James O. Siegert for sharing his knowledge of
oil wells and the industry.

Sarah Schroeder for answering questions
about Houston.

Shelley Utz, hairstylist.

Randy Rychlik, paramedic.

And Vicki Cowan for her keen eye.

All errors are strictly mine.

Chapter One

The fierce afternoon wind whipped through the landscape like an errant child of Mother Nature, set on doing some damage. Heavy, dark clouds from the north threatened rain, a sure sign that the old lady had not finished her wrath of winter.

Chance Hardin hated March.

And all the agonizing memories it stirred.

He shifted uneasily at the kitchen table on the High Five ranch in High Cotton, Texas, and forced his eyes away from the window. Gripping his warm coffee cup, he stared into its murky depths, seeing a night as dark as the brew inside. Through the blackness the emotions of a twelve-year-old boy surfaced—a boy whose world had been shattered by loud voices, screams—and death.

On a miserable March night.

Chance felt his stomach twist into a knot as his brothers waited. He'd been avoiding this conversation for twenty-two years. How much longer could he stall?

"Come on, Chance." Cadde was putting on the pressure, just like Chance knew he would. It was part of being an older brother. "You know Dad wanted us to work together."

You didn't really know him.

"Yeah." Cisco, his middle brother, nick-named Kid, joined in. "The oil business is in our blood. We've all been involved in the industry. Now, thanks to Roscoe Murdock, Cadde owns a big part of Shilah Oil. Of course, there were strings attached, but that didn't stop ol' Cadde." Kid slapped Cadde on the back and received a knockout glare in return, that didn't faze him one bit. "Come on, Chance, we can be the bosses, setting the pace and making Shilah Oil one of the best companies in Texas."

Chance raised his head. "Roscoe's daughter, Jessie, owns the biggest part, and she'll be calling the shots."

He didn't know why he felt a need to remind his brothers of that, but the whole inheritance thing was a bit of a shock. Not that Cadde hadn't earned it. He had.

Roscoe had been paranoid about Jessie's safety ever since his niece had been kidnapped and murdered. After the tragedy he'd had Jessie guarded twenty-four hours a day. Cadde had told Chance that Jessie was seven at the time, and now she had to be close to thirty.

Even though she was a fully grown woman, Roscoe didn't let up on his protection of Jessie. On his deathbed he'd made a deal with Cadde, who had been his right hand at Shilah. If Cadde married Jessie and promised to protect her, Roscoe would make him CEO of the oil company and sign over a portion of his shares. Roscoe just forgot to mention that his daughter would inherit the biggest part of Shilah Oil, the company Roscoe and his brother, Al, had started in the forties.

Chance had met Jessie a couple of times when he'd visited Cadde in Houston. She was a petite, dark-haired, dark-eyed beauty, and he could see why Cadde had no problem with the arrangement. Not that Chance knew much about it—Cadde's marriage was his business.

He just didn't figure his brother as the marriage-of-convenience type. Although Cadde would do anything to further his career in the oil industry. It had been his dream since they were kids.

It had been the dream of their father.

"I can handle Jessie."

Chance came back to the conversation with a start, but kept his emotions in check, as always. Fiddling with his cup, he had to admit that Cadde could probably handle Jessie— the way he handled everything in life, with his confident, can-do-anything air. Just like Kid, Cadde was unstoppable when he had his mind set on something.

"We need you, Chance. Your skill with the rigs is better than that of anyone I know. I want to try the new drilling techniques on some of the old leases, to give those fields a jump start. You're the man to oversee the job."

Chance swallowed hard. "I'm happy at Southern Cross."

Cadde leaned forward, resting his forearms on the table, his chair making a scraping noise on the tiled floor. "Why don't you just admit that you still blame Kid and me for the accident?"

The kitchen became painfully quiet. Talking about that horrible night was something they never did. The wrought-iron clock on the wall ticked away precious seconds. Aunt Etta moved from the kitchen counter to stand a few feet from the table, a wooden spoon in her grasp just in case she had to break up a fight, much as she had when they were boys.

A hand lightly touched Chance's shoulder—a gesture from Uncle Rufus, telling him to keep his cool. Their elderly aunt and uncle had taken the Hardin boys in after their parents' tragic deaths, and knew them better than anyone.

"I never blamed you," Chance said clearly and without emotion. That night was too heartbreaking to think about, but he could feel the memory slicing into his brain with a sharp edge of reality. His parents had been returning home to High Cotton from an out-of-town basketball game of Cadde's and Cisco's.

Chuck Hardin had pulled two shifts on an oil rig and then had taken his wife and Chance to the game because his sons had wanted him at the state championship. Speculation was he'd fallen asleep at the wheel. Chance knew differently. Dozing in the backseat, he was the only one who'd survived that fatal crash as the car had swerved, left the road and hit a tree. And the only one who knew what had really happened that night.

He planned to take that secret to the grave.

Cadde eased back, his dark eyes pinned on Chance. All three brothers had the deep brown eyes of their father. "You've been different ever since. Distant. Getting anything out of you is like pulling teeth."

Chance didn't squirm. He met Cadde's stare. "Losing one's parents can change a person."

"Yeah," Kid interjected in a nostalgic tone. "We've all changed, but it's time for us to be family again—the Hardin boys taking on the world."

That sounded good to Chance, but he couldn't weaken. Guilt beat at him like a persistent hangover. If he spent more time around his brothers, he wouldn't be able to keep his secret. Telling them would destroy their love and trust of their father, as it had destroyed his. He wouldn't do that—ever.

Uncle Rufus stood. In his seventies, bow-legged and a cowboy to the core, Rufus Johns spoke little, but when he did, they listened. He and Aunt Etta had worked for the High Five ranch since they were teenagers, and lived in a small house not far from the big house, as they called the Belle residence on the ranch. Now Rufus, as he'd been many times when they'd lived with him, was again their mediator.

"Your brothers asked you a question. It requires a simple yes or no. What's your answer?"

Chance clenched his jaw and willed himself to relax. "No. I have a good job at Southern Cross and I'm not interested in leaving it for the oil business...just yet."

"Damn it." Cadde hit the table with his fist, making the coffee cups rattle.

Aunt Etta tapped his shoulder with her spoon. "You're not too old for me to use this on, you know. Respect your brother's decision. You and Kid can get into enough trouble on your own."

Cadde hooked an arm around Etta's thin waist and pulled her to his side. "Aunt Etta, Chance is missing out on the biggest opportunity of his life."

"That's his choice."

"I just..."

Cadde's words trailed away as five-year-old Kira Yates burst through the back door, followed by her parents, Skylar and Cooper.

Kira eyed the two strangers and edged her way over to Chance. "Look what I drew in school." She handed him the paper. It was a child's drawing of a family.

Chance introduced his brothers to Kira.

"I'm gonna have a brother, too." Kira pointed proudly to the picture.

"I see. Very good."

Kira carried the picture to Etta.

"What a little artist you are." The elderly woman kissed the top of her head. "Miss Dorie is waiting for you in the parlor."

"Gotta go." Kira darted away.

Sky, the youngest Belle daughter and five months pregnant, walked over to the table. "My, my, the Hardin boys are back in town. Lock up your daughters, folks. They can't be trusted."

Kid got to his feet and hugged her. "Dane used to say that all the time." He, Cadde and Chance had grown up with the Belle sisters, and Dane Belle had been like the father they'd lost.

Sky winked. "Especially to his daughters."

Kid rocked back on his heels with the crafty grin of a possum eating honey. "Have no idea why."

Of all the brothers, he hid his pain in

humor and romancing the ladies. He was well known for it. Cadde was the driven one, set on making his dream come true. Chance, on the other hand, buried himself behind a veil of secrecy. The accident had affected all their lives, one way or another.

Cadde rose and hugged Sky and shook Cooper's hand. "I heard you're the owner of High Five now." When Cooper had allowed himself to fall in love with Sky, he'd decided to stay in High Cotton forever, so he'd approached Caitlyn and Maddie, the other two sisters, with an offer they couldn't refuse.

"Yep, and I heard you're the owner of an oil company." Cadde, Cooper and Judd Calhoun, owner of Southern Cross, were about the same age and had gone to school together, along with Maddie's husband, Walker. High Cotton was a close-knit community of family and friends.

Cadde nodded. "I guess we've grown up."

"Sobering, isn't it?" Cooper replied, while shaking Kid's hand. "Still riding shotgun?" Cadde and Kid were fourteen months apart, and so close, people often thought they were twins. The humorous Kid always kept the deep and brooding Cadde in line with his antics, or more accurately, kept him on his toes.

"Yeah." Kid's infectious grin widened. "Someone has to keep an eye on Cadde or he gets a little too intense."

"Daddy, Mommy," Kira called from the parlor. "Gran's waiting. We're having a tea party." Dorthea Belle was the matriarch of the family and everyone loved her. Just as her son, Dane had, she made the orphaned Hardin boys feel like family.

"This could take a while." Cooper delivered the words with a Texas-size smile. Family suited the man. "Stay as long as you want and visit."

As Cooper left, Chance reached for his hat. "I've got to get back. Judd and Cait are gone for a week and I don't want to stay away too long."

"Damn." Kid snapped his fingers. "I was hoping to see Caitlyn."

Chance sighed. "You can't flirt with her like you used to or Judd will give you a king-size headache."

Kid shook his head. "Can't believe she finally married him."

Caitlyn was the oldest Belle daughter and Kid had always hit on her. Hell, he hit on all the sisters—that was his nature. He never met a woman he didn't like. The Belles never missed a chance to set him straight. They'd lived so close they were like brothers and sisters—and they'd fought like siblings. Cait would vow never to speak to Kid again. In the next instant they'd be racing their horses to the general store, or off across the nearest pasture, argument forgotten.

Chance had thought that Cait would never leave the place of her birth, but love was a powerful force. Her marrying her archenemy from the neighboring ranch came as a surprise to everyone, except Chance and her sisters. Since her teens, Cait had been in love with Judd, but it had taken years for them to work out their differences.

Even though Chance and Cait talked a lot, he'd never told her his secret. He'd never told anyone.

"Give it a rest, Kid," Cadde said. "You were never serious about any of the Belles. They were family."

"That's what made it so much fun," he replied with that silly grin. "They knew I wasn't serious. You know how Caitlyn is when she's mad? With just a frown, she can make a grown man take ten steps backward without even thinking or blinking. Hell, I had fun getting her angry."

Etta gave him a strange look. "Sometimes I worry about you, boy."

Kid hugged her. "Ah, Aunt Etta, I'm just joking. You know me. I'd never touch one of Dane's daughters. Hell, he'd have killed me, but that didn't keep me from teasing them."

"Yeah." She pointed a finger in his face. "You leave the girls alone. They're happily married, with babies."

"Pay no attention to him, Aunt Etta," Cadde told her. "He's always about a pint short on his blood supply."

"Now wait a minute…"

Cadde ignored Kid and turned to Chance. "The offer is still on the table. Think it over. We want you with us."

Chance nodded and walked out. As he got into his truck, he couldn't deny that the offer was tempting. When they were younger, their father would say he didn't want them toiling in the oil fields all their lives like he had. That as brothers working together, they could accomplish anything—be the bosses, not hands. That's why Chance never saw what was to come—the horrible truth. The man who'd spouted family values, loyalty and love was a phony. His other two sons still idolized him. So how could Chance destroy that illusion?

With his jaw clenched, he turned from High Five onto the blacktop county road that led to the Southern Cross ranch. When Judd had offered him the job of foreman, Chance had been happy for the opportunity to cowboy again. He was tired of the grime and muck working as a roughneck, and wanted to settle down for a while. Also, Aunt Etta and Uncle Rufus were getting older, and he thought they might need him close by.

The Hardin home place was about a mile beyond the Southern Cross. Chance was glad he didn't have to ride past it every day, but there were times when he was checking fences and he'd glance across the road and see the small, white frame house nestled among the oak trees. His pulse would quicken and nausea would gnaw at his insides for a second.

None of the brothers had been inside the house since that fatal night. Dane and his cowboys had moved all their clothes and belongings into Aunt Etta and Uncle Ru's spare bedroom. In that tiny room they'd grieved, bonded tighter and learned to live again—all thanks to Dane Belle.

After a week of them not knowing what to do with themselves, Dane had said, "Boys, you've been dealt a mighty blow—some men would break under the sadness and pressure. But as a tribute to your parents you have to show you're Hardin stock, tough and unbreakable." He had given them a moment to digest that, and then added, "Let's go. There're cows to be fed."

When they weren't in school, Dane had kept them busy. They'd thrived on his attention. He'd taught them how to cowboy and how to be tough. Dane was a gambler and they'd all benefited when he won big. When Cadde graduated from high school, Dane had bought him a brand-new Chevy pickup. Aunt Etta had said it was too much, and Uncle Ru had agreed.

Cadde had held his breath as he'd waited for Dane to talk them into allowing him to keep the gift. And he had. Cadde had left for Texas Tech University in Lubbock to get a petroleum engineering degree. The next year Kid had followed in his own new truck.

Dane's daughters had different mothers, so Maddie and Skylar lived out of state and spent holidays and summers on the ranch. Caitlyn was the only sister raised on High Five. With Chance's brothers gone, that had left him and Cait. They'd graduated together.

And just like his brothers, Chance got a truck. Cait got a car.

She'd been furious, for she'd wanted a truck, too. Dane had said that women don't drive trucks—they drive cars. For a solid month she'd refused to drive the car, but eventually gave in.

Dane's gambling and drinking took a downward spiral in his later years, and he'd passed away. It was a blow to everyone at High Five, to the community, and to the Hardin boys. Chance supposed everyone had to die. He just wished he didn't think about it so much.

Dane would be pleased to know that his girls were all happy, and living in High Cotton. Maddie had married Walker, the constable, and they had three kids. Cait and Judd had twin boys. Dane's wild daughter, Sky, was expecting her second child. Dane was surely resting in peace.

Chance just wished…

The brutal wind tugged at the three-quarter-ton truck as if it were a play toy. Spring was knocking on winter's door, but winter, Mother Nature's stepchild, was set on claiming more time. She would soon tire, though. Calving season was around the corner at the ranch and Chance would be busy. He wouldn't have time for a lot of thinking, especially about his brother's offer.

But as he drove steadily homeward, he had to wonder how long he could continue to keep his secret.

Could a Hardin be that strong?

Shay Dumont glanced at the directions in her hand while keeping an eye on the road. Southern Cross couldn't be much farther. Miles of ranch land with thick woods and swaying grasses flashed by. She chewed on a nail, then forced herself to stop the bad habit. But here she was, on this lonely road in the middle of nowhere. It was a little unnerving.

What she had planned was unnerving, too.

How much farther could it be? Then she saw the huge stone entrance and the wrought-iron arc with the name Southern Cross welded on it. Bingo! This was it. Her heart raced and her clammy hands gripped the steering wheel. She'd waited years for this day, and nerves weren't going to get the best of her.

The Calhouns were going to get the shock of their lives. Her mother had told her to enjoy every minute of the confrontation, but she'd never enjoyed hurting anyone. That wasn't Shay's nature.

She passed the entrance. For the first time she realized how hard this was going to be. Taking a deep breath, she looked for a place to turn around. Pasture lands stretched on either side of her, enclosed with barbed wire fences. No Trespassing signs were attached to the wire every half mile or so.

Before she could maneuver the car to the side of the road, her cell phone buzzed. She reached in her purse for it and clicked On.

"Have you reached the ranch?"

"Yes." Just what she needed—her mother giving her more instructions. Shay let out a long breath, made a U-turn and drove back, the wind giving her an extra push.

"You know what you have to do."

"You don't have to remind me." Shay tried to hide the bite in her voice, but failed. "How's Darcy?"

"She's in the living room with Nettie. The quicker you get back here the better. That kid is getting on my nerves with her loud, squeaky voice. Why you took her in is still beyond me."

Shay's knuckles turned white from gripping the wheel. She was the legal guardian of eight-year-old Darcy Stevens. Shay and Darcy's mother, Beth, had been very good friends. When Beth, a single mom, had asked her to be her daughter's guardian if anything ever happened to her, Shay had agreed. In their twenties, neither had dreamed that tragedy might strike them so young, but it had. Beth was diagnosed with pancreatic cancer, and had died within months.

Darcy was filled with so much anger at her mother's death that Shay was at a loss sometimes about how to deal with her. She sucked at being a mother.

"I'll be back as quick as I can. She does fine with Nettie," Shay replied. Her mother's cousin, who lived next door, was a lifesaver.

"Avoid that Hardin boy who's the foreman. He could be trouble."

"I don't plan on talking to any of the cowboys." A Hardin was the last person she wanted to meet.

"Don't you let me down."

Shay clicked off with the words ringing in her ears. They epitomized her whole life. Her mother had probably started saying them to her in the crib. Where most kids had cereal for breakfast, Shay had been spoon-fed guilt.

She did not have a Cosby kid's childhood. It was more like a Hallmark afternoon special.

But today she was going to make up for a lot of that.

By doing exactly what her mother wanted.

What *was* she doing? Shay's mind reeled with unsettling thoughts, and she misjudged the distance to her purse. Her cell phone fell to the floor. Reaching for it, she turned the wheel too far, and the car slid off the road. Quickly overcorrecting, she glanced up and saw a silver truck heading straight for her. She jerked the wheel and the car left the road and barreled across a bar ditch, through a fence, and kept going.

She screamed when a tree came out of nowhere. Frantically, she jammed her foot on the brake, and the car spun, her head hitting the wheel. A searing pain shot through her, followed by a soft white light and then darkness.

Chance pulled over to the side of the road and jumped out, poking 911 into his cell. He gave his name, location and a few details. The wind tugged at his hat, so he threw it into the backseat.

The operator told him there was a bad

wreck on US 290 and that all available ambulances were en route there. She said she'd send one as soon as she could. As they spoke, Chance paused briefly on the shoulder of the road and took in the situation. The car had crashed through a fence, grazed a tree and was resting in the creek.

"Can you see anything?" the dispatcher asked.

"Yes. The car is in Crooked Creek."

"I've notified the volunteer fire department in your area and the constable. Help is on the way. Check and see if anyone is injured."

Clutching his phone, Chance ran down the slope and leaped over the ditch. *Please, not another wreck on a dreary March day,* was all he could think.

"A small Chevy is slowly taking in water," he reported to the dispatcher. He stepped into the creek to take a closer look. "Only one person in the car—a woman. Her head is resting against the steering wheel."

"Does she have on her seat belt?"

Chance peered inside. "Yes."

"Air bag inflated?"

"No."

"Do you see blood?"

"No. But there's water on the floorboard

and it's rising." His eyes shifted to the front of the car. "Steam is coming from under the hood, but I expect that's from the hot motor hitting water."

"Yes, probably. Can you open the door?"

"Just a sec." Shoving his cell into his jeans pocket, he grabbed the handle and yanked on it. "No. It's jammed and the water is holding it tight," he said, anxious moments later. The wind whipped the water against his legs and tousled his hair. His efforts on the door made the car inch farther into the creek.

Damn!

Memories beat at him. His mother's blonde hair covered in blood flashed through his mind. Chance hadn't been able to save her. But he would save this woman.

"Do you hear a siren?"

"No. Not yet."

"Try the other doors."

He did as instructed, but none would open. "They won't budge, and the water is rising. It's up to her waist. Where in the hell is everyone?"

"An ambulance has been rerouted from US 290, but that's twenty miles away. High Cotton is one of those remote communities we have problems with, but the fire department should be there."

"They're not." Chance bent and gazed in at the unconscious woman again. Her blonde hair was long and the tips were now touching water. "This lady doesn't have a lot of time."

"Okay. I just heard from High Cotton's fire chief. They're having trouble with the truck."

"Damn." They were always having problems with that old fire engine. They'd been having fundraisers for a new one and had applied for a grant from the state of Texas to help with the cost. But this lady needed help now.

"Just stay on the line."

"I'm not going anywhere, but this car is filling up fast."

"Okay. Do you have anything to break a window?"

"I have a crowbar in my truck."

"Get it, and wait for instructions."

Gulping a breath, he ran back to his truck for the implement, then sloshed back into the creek to the stranded vehicle. "Now what?" he asked, though he already knew the answer.

"Break the driver's side window, but be careful."

Switching to speakerphone, he placed his

cell on the roof of the car, then looked inside again. The driver was still out cold, leaning toward the right, that was good. She was farther away from the door.

With one swing, he shattered the window. Luckily, it broke into a sheet of tiny cubes and he was able to break it away from the frame. Pieces of glass fell into the water and others dropped into the car. As he worked, sweat rolled down his face despite the relentless wind.

"It's done," he said.

"Check and see if she has a pulse."

He brushed her long hair aside and felt the smooth skin of her neck. A faint rhythm beat against his fingers and he let out a long breath. "Yes, she's alive."

"No help yet?"

"No, and the wind is not helping. The car is not stable."

"Can you get her out?"

Chance took another deep breath. "I'll try."

"Just be sure to brace her neck."

After making sure there were no jagged glass edges left in the window frame, he reached in, stuck his hand in the water and felt for her seat belt. It made a swishing sound as it slid back into its holder. With a grunt, he grasped her under her armpits and tugged, maneuvering carefully to pull her through the window. The buoyancy of the water helped. At one point the car swayed, and he held his breath.

Finally clear, Chance braced her head on his chest and dragged her away, leaving a wet trail in the mud.

He gently laid her on the grass. While supporting her neck, he managed to struggle out of his wet shirt and stuff it under her head. Then he hurried back for his phone.

"What's happening? Can you hear me?" he heard the dispatcher calling.

"I have her out on the creek bank." He knelt beside the unconscious woman. "She has a slight gash on her forehead."

"Is she bleeding?"

"Not much." He glanced toward the sky and saw the dark thunderclouds gaining force. "Where in the hell is that ambulance? It's fixing to rain."

"Stay calm."

"Listen, this woman needs to get out of the weather."

"Check her arms and legs to see if anything is broken."

He ran his hands over her limbs. "Doesn't

seem to be and I can't see any more blood." He made a quick decision. "I'll take her to the Southern Cross ranch a mile down the road. Route the ambulance there."

"They're about ten minutes away."

Raindrops fell on his hand. "We don't have ten minutes."

"Okay. Just be careful with her neck."

"I will." Losing no time, Chance shoved his phone into his back pocket again and gingerly scooped her into his arms, making sure her head was braced against his shoulder. As he started toward his truck, he heard a swooshing sound and turned to see the car submerged in the water, with only the roof showing.

Staggering in his wet boots and jeans, he climbed onto the road and hurried to the vehicle. After depositing her on the passenger side, he repositioned his shirt beneath her head, then tilted the seat back. Blood covered her forehead, but the gash had stopped bleeding. Her skin was pasty white and her hair seemed to be everywhere.

He fished his phone out of his pocket. "Thanks for your help. We're on the way to Southern Cross."

"The woman was lucky to have you around.

Good luck. The ambulance should be there shortly."

As soon as he clicked off, the cell buzzed again. It was Walker, the constable. Finally.

"Hey, Chance. I've been at the courthouse in Giddings and I just got the news about the wreck. How's the driver?"

Chance glanced at her. "She's still out and I'm taking her to Southern Cross. The volunteer fire department sure didn't help."

"Henry couldn't get the truck started. It's time the community did something about that or we're going to have a major fire and the whole town is going to suffer."

"Yeah." Chance snapped the woman's seat belt into place and ran around the truck, his boots sloshing. He crawled into the driver's seat, still talking to Walker. "Maybe this will encourage everyone in High Cotton to get behind the project."

"We can only hope. I'm on my way."

Within minutes Chance rolled into the driveway of the ranch. He called Renee, Judd's mother, to announce his arrival with a casualty.

Renee opened the door at once. "Oh, good heavens, come in," she said as he carried the patient up the steps. Thunder rumbled in warning and heavy rain began to fall. He'd made it just in time.

"My boots and jeans are wet and muddy, Renee," Chance said apologetically.

"Not a problem! I can clean up a little mud," she said.

Chance wiped his boots on the mat as best he could, then carried his load inside. Renee spread sheets on the sofa in the den and he gingerly laid the unconscious woman on them.

"What happened?" Renee asked, glancing from one bedraggled figure to the other.

"She ran off the road into Crooked Creek and I had to pull her out. I've already called 911 and Walker."

"Good heavens."

Chance pointed to the woman's face. "She has a cut on her head."

"I'll get some supplies."

As Renee hurried away, the woman stirred. "Oh, o-o-oh."

"Lie still," Chance instructed. "You've been in an accident."

Renee came back and cleaned the cut with warm water and applied a bandage. "That should hold you until the paramedics arrive."

Their patient looked around and Chance

noticed her eyes were green, a startlingly brilliant color. The kind of eyes that caught a man off guard with their intensity and beauty. She was pretty, too, with a pert nose, clear classic features and gorgeous blond hair streaked with a lighter color he was sure was artificially produced. Definitely not a country girl. She had a big city look about her, and he wondered what she was doing around here.

"Where am I?" Shay blinked, feeing disoriented.

Someone patted her arm. "Don't you fret, sugar. You're fine. The paramedics should be here soon." It was a woman's voice, sure and confident, with a Southern drawl.

Paramedics?

"You're at the Southern Cross ranch," a male voice said. Shay glanced up to see a handsome man with wet, disheveled hair staring down at her. His face was lean, his muscled body was showcased in a white T-shirt, tight jeans and cowboy boots. A cowboy? His eyes were like dark chocolate, tempting, sinful and good for her heart. Had she died and gone to heaven, and was he her reward for putting up with all the crap in her life? Oh, he was a very good reward. Now she felt giddy and...

What did he say?

Southern Cross?

She tried to sit up, winced and lay back as pain ripped through her head. "What happened?"

"You were in an accident, sugar," the woman said.

"You ran your car off the road into Crooked Creek," the cowboy added.

Bits and pieces fitted together in Shay's head like one of Darcy's puzzles. "A silver truck was headed straight for me. I tried…"

"That was me, and I was on my side of the road." His voice was deep and commanding, with a Texas accent much like Matthew McConaughey's, but delivered with an edge of censure. That rankled, even if the sound set off unexpected waves of pleasure.

Shay narrowed her eyes, then winced. "You ran me onto the shoulder."

"You did that all by yourself."

"Now let's don't quibble." The woman intervened, as if used to dealing with cantankerous children. "I'm Renee Calhoun and this is Chance Hardin, the foreman of Southern Cross."

Renee Calhoun.
Chance Hardin.

Oh, no! This just wasn't her day. The names

settled in Shay's stomach like sour milk. Now what should she do?

The woman who had broken up her parents' marriage was a couple of feet away. Shay squinted at her. She seemed perfectly normal, dressed in a cream linen blouse and pants. Her dyed blonde hair hung like a bell around an attractive face. From her mother's description, Shay had expected Renee to have horns and a tail, next-of-kin to the devil.

Maybe this was good luck, Shay thought. She had a foot inside the house, and soon, when she'd regained her equilibrium, she'd tell this hellish woman a thing or two.

The cowboy looked down at her with those dark, dark eyes and she resisted the urge to wriggle. What was he thinking? It was hard to tell, since the blackness of his eyes seemed to block out his emotions as if he were wearing sunglasses. Did he know who she was? Of course not. Shay was getting paranoid. She couldn't think about Chance Hardin.

She looked around the room. Cathedral ceilings with wagon wheel chandeliers met her gaze. The walls were a rich mahogany done in a picture-framing style. Photos of Judd Calhoun, his wife and twin sons took pride of place. A huge stone fireplace covered one wall and was adorned with a rustic Texas star. A wedding photo of Renee and Jack Calhoun graced the intricately carved wood mantel.

Shay stared at the man—her father—and felt no emotion other than anger. How could she? She'd never known him. He'd kicked her mother out when he'd met Renee, his first wife, and wanted to remarry her. He didn't even care that Blanche was pregnant.

For so many years Shay had dreamed of being here, inside Southern Cross, to get a glimpse of where she should have been raised. But oddly, and fittingly, she felt out of place. This wasn't Huckleberry Lane, where she lived with her mother and Darcy.

Thoughts of the little girl filled her aching head. Darcy didn't like being alone with Blanche, and Shay had to let her know she'd be back soon.

"May I have my purse, please?"

Renee and Chance exchanged a glance.

"It was in your car," the cowboy said.

"I know. I need to make a call."

"You don't remember?"

"What?" Why was he talking as if she were five years old?

"After I pulled you out, the Chevy sank

into Crooked Creek. I'm sure everything in your purse is ruined."

Oh, no! She'd just paid off her car loan and now the vehicle was gone. A wave of regret washed over her. She should never have let Blanche talk her into this. Jack Calhoun was dead and nothing could change the past. Shay had to get out of here and fast.

"What's your name, sugar?" Renee asked in a kind, soothing voice. Shay hated that.

Spit fire or something. Please don't be nice. She caught the cowboy's eyes. Chance Hardin's concerned gaze was doing a number on her resolve. And her conscience.

"Shay," she replied, her voice low.

"How pretty." Renee patted her arm again. "For a pretty young lady."

For some reason tears stung the back of her eyes. Her mother had never called her pretty or ever paid her a compliment. The gesture coming from Renee Calhoun was almost too much, on top of everything else that happened on this horrendous day.

"Thank you," she managed to answer, before the sound of a siren startled her. "What's that?"

"An ambulance. You need medical attention. I'll open the front door."

Renee walked away and Shay stared at Chance. She didn't have any choice but to enlist his help—a Hardin's help. Why did he have to be here?

"Please, I'm fine. I don't need an ambulance."

"You probably have a concussion."

She forced herself to sit up.

He practically leaped to her side. "Whoa. You shouldn't have done that."

She frowned, which made her head hurt that much more. "What?"

"You shouldn't have sat up until the paramedics arrived."

"I'm fine, really." Brushing her hair from her face, she wondered what had happened to her hair clip. And she realized for the first time that she was wet. Damn! Chance must have saved her life. Just what she needed— more guilt. Forcing negative thoughts aside, she appealed to him. "I don't have health insurance and I can't afford an ambulance or a hospital bill."

The candor in her voice got to Chance— and the fear. What was she afraid of?

"I'm sure you can make payment arrangements."

She laughed, a sound like a frightened

child's. "I don't have any extra money and…" Her voice trailed off as two paramedics wheeled in a stretcher.

One medic checked Shay's pulse and blood pressure, then took her temperature. Next he removed Renee's bandage and studied the cut. "Doesn't look bad," he said as he applied ointment and another bandage.

"I'm fine," Shay insisted.

The man shone a small penlight into her eyes and asked her to follow his finger.

While the paramedic continue to examine her, Chance moved away to speak to Renee. "She doesn't have health insurance and doesn't want to go to the hospital."

"Well, hell, I'll pay the bill," the older woman offered. "She needs help."

Shay overheard her and axed that idea immediately. "No. No. You're not paying the bill. I'm fine. I'm not going to a hospital."

Renee pulled Chance farther aside and whispered, "What do you have in mind?"

"Can she stay here tonight? I'll get her a rental car first thing in the morning."

"If the paramedics say she's okay, I don't see why not."

The attendant stepped back with his hands

on his hips. "It would be best to go to the hospital and get checked out."

"I'm fine, really," Shay replied again in that nervous tone.

"What do you think?" Chance asked the man.

"She can focus and her eyes are clear, so I suppose if she refuses to go we can't make her. But if she grows dizzy or passes out, you need to get her to a hospital."

"We will," he promised.

The medic looked at Shay. "Stay awake for a while and see your doctor as soon as possible."

"Okay."

As the ambulance left, Renee said, "Well, it looks as if I have a houseguest. Just give me a few minutes and I'll get you some dry clothes." She hurried away, her shoes tapping on the hardwood floor.

Shay glanced at Chance, her eyes huge in her pale face. "Thank you."

She managed to look coy, inviting and desperate all at the same time. His heart knocked against his ribs like a bronc about to be broken. "You're welcome." He swallowed hard, this unexpected attraction hitting him like a sucker punch. His next words came out terse.

"What's your last name? And your auto insurance company?"

"Excuse me?"

"I'll make some calls for you so I can get
you a rental in the morning. But I need information."

She seemed to hesitate. "Stevens," she finally answered. "But I'll call my insurance
company."

Fear still tinged her voice, and Chance
knew something wasn't quite right. "Fine.
You can use the phone in your bedroom."

"Okay, but I really need to go home."

A reasonable request. Maybe he was making something out of nothing. "You said you
wanted to call someone?"

Shay chewed on a fingernail. "Yes. I'll
use the phone in the bedroom to check on
my mother. She's dying of lung cancer and a
cousin takes care of her when I'm not there."

Chance was taken aback at the turmoil in
the young woman's life, and against his better
judgment he could feel himself being pulled
into her problems. Before he could form a response, the doorbell rang.

He handed her his cell. "Call your mother.
I'll make sure you get home tomorrow."

"Thank you," Shay replied, quickly punching in a number as he walked to the door.

Walker stood on the threshold. "Is the woman okay?"

Chance stepped out onto the veranda. "She's a little shaken up and refuses to go to the E.R."

"The volunteer fire department is now at the site. Henry finally got the truck running. Since the rain is letting up, a wrecker is also there to pull the car out. I'm pretty sure it's totaled." The constable pulled his Stetson low to keep the wind from taking it, and glanced over Chance's wet appearance. "Sorry you had to deal with that."

Everyone knew of his parents' deaths. It had happened on the same county road, closer to Giddings. Though only twelve, Chance had worked valiantly to get his parents out—but they were already dead.

"I've developed Teflon feelings," he joked.

"Yeah, right." Clearly, Walker didn't believe him for a minute. "You get any information from her?"

"She said her name is Shay Stevens."

Walker frowned. "That's strange. The license plate must not have been secured properly, because I found it in the grass. I ran a check with the Department of Public Safety just in case she was still unconscious, and it's registered to Shay Dumont from Houston."

"Hmm." Chance rubbed his jaw in thought. That name ran a bell, but he couldn't place it. That niggling feeling returned. The lady wasn't who she said she was. He felt a moment of regret. He was beginning to like her. Now he had some questions and was determined to get answers—one way or another.

Who was she?

And what did she want in High Cotton, Texas?

Chapter Two

Chance went upstairs to talk to Shay, but Renee was hovering around and he didn't get an opportunity. He didn't want Renee to think something was wrong, so he headed out the door for dry clothes and boots.

"Thank you for pulling me out of the car," Shay said in a rush before he left. "Your cell is downstairs."

"Thanks." He turned to look at her. She sat on the side of the bed in a white fluffy robe of Renee's. Nervousness, shock and fear flitted across her pretty face. What was causing her such anguish? He didn't have time to figure it out. He had to get into dry clothes and check on the cowboys. Work awaited him and he had to go. *Who are you?* He planned to find out later when Renee wasn't around.

Renee followed him to the kitchen. "I think I'll fix her a bite to eat."

"Missing the kids, huh?"

"You bet. I can't wait for the twins to come home."

Chance thought for a moment and asked, "Do you mind if I spend the night in the house? I'm a little leery of you being alone with a stranger." He had a room at the bunkhouse, but that niggling feeling wouldn't go away. He had brought the woman here and he had to make sure Renee was safe.

"What do you think?" Renee whispered. "That she's going to murder me in my bed?"

He shrugged. "I just have a strange feeling. That's all."

"Then by all means, sleep in the house."

"Thanks. I'll be back later."

When he returned the woman was asleep in a guest room. Should she be sleeping? It had been almost two hours since the medics left, so he supposed it was okay. The light was on and she was curled up in bed with a wistful expression on her face, blonde hair all around her. She was probably the most beautiful woman he'd ever seen. Why did they have to meet under these circumstances? This stranger was hiding something and he had to be on guard.

Walker dropped by later to talk to Shay about the accident. Chance told him she was asleep, and the constable said he'd come back in the morning. The car had been towed into Giddings, he reported, and he'd brought the sodden remains of Shay's purse. Since it had been filled with muddy water, Walker had done his best to dry it out, but everything was ruined. The only thing legible on her driver's license was her name—Shay Dumont.

Where had he heard that name before? Chance went to bed with it rattling around in his head, and again he vowed to get answers.

At six he woke up, slipped into his jeans and a T-shirt and headed downstairs to make coffee. Since the Calhouns were gone, the housekeeper was on vacation, too. His plan was to carry a cup to the woman and talk.

As he finished making the coffee, the phone rang. He grabbed the wall phone before it woke up everyone. Renee was not an early riser.

"You ordered a rental?"

"Yes."

"I have to deliver it early because I'm the only one working the lot today."

"Okay. What time?"

"I'm here now."

"Oh. I'll be right out." Chance marched to the door and opened it. A middle-aged man stood there with a clipboard, which he held out to Chance, who scribbled his name. "This was fast," he commented.

"Ms. Dumont's insurance agent called late yesterday. He'd gotten photos from the wrecker service via the internet and it was a done deal. The car will be scrapped." The man handed over a receipt and the keys. About that time an older truck with loud exhaust pipes pulled in.

"That's my son. Gotta go."

"Thanks," Chance called to the man's retreating back.

He hurried into the kitchen for coffee. Placing the keys and receipt on the granite kitchen island, he poured a cup. After taking a sip he decided he'd better put on his boots and shirt before talking to the woman.

Swinging around, he came to a halt. Shay was standing in the doorway, fully dressed in the clothes she'd worn yesterday, the bandage still on her forehead. Her long hair glistened in the kitchen light.

He swallowed. "How are you?" he managed to ask her.

"Fine." She held out her arms. "Renee washed and dried my clothes. Wasn't that nice?"

"Renee's a nice lady."

Shay didn't respond to that. Instead she waved a hand toward the coffeepot. "May I have some?"

"Sure." Her sudden appearance had made him forget his manners. He poured a cup and handed it to her. In the process he noticed that her fingernails were bitten down to the quick. Obviously she was a very nervous person.

She took a tentative sip. "Do you live here?"

She was fishing for information, and Chance was willing to give her only so much. But it was hard to stick to that resolve with her green eyes so inviting.

"No. My gig's at the bunkhouse, but I stayed in the house last night to make sure… you were okay."

"That's so sweet." She touched his bare arm and tiny sizzles of pleasure radiated through him. "Oh." She spotted the keys and receipt on the island. "They brought my rental?"

"Yes. It's outside."

"That was quick." Setting her cup down, she slipped the keys into the front pocket of her jeans, folded the receipt and stuffed it into her back pocket.

He watched her every movement and thought how graceful and beautiful she was. The knit top outlined her breasts and the tight jeans emphasized her slim curves. He cleared his throat. "Walker, the constable, brought your purse and phone from your car." He pointed. "They're in that plastic bag on the floor."

"Oh." She knelt and examined the contents. "Good grief, everything's covered in mud."

"I'm afraid it's pretty much ruined."

"Yeah," she murmured, removing her driver's license, a credit card and some cash. She stuffed them into her other pocket and stood, wiping her hands on her jeans. "Do you mind throwing the rest away?"

"No problem."

Silence followed as they faced each other. Chance could feel the tension building in the room. He had to admit he was attracted to her, and he wished he'd dressed before coming down. The situation was a little too intimate. But the doubts kept his emotions in check.

She glanced around the kitchen. "I'd like to thank whoever lives in this big house."

And the doubts doubled. She wanted information.

"Renee's son and his family live here."

"I'd like to thank them."

The tension tripled. "There's no need."

She was about to persist when his phone buzzed. He reached for it in his pocket and saw the caller ID. "I'm sorry, but I have to take this."

"I'll just...go up and thank Renee." Shay picked up her cup.

"Walker, the constable, is coming by to talk to you this morning," Chance called as she left.

"Okay."

He clicked on his phone. "What is it, Monty?" Monty was one of the cowboys on the ranch.

"Where are you? You didn't sleep in the bunkhouse last night."

"Did the boys fix the fence at Crooked Creek?" Chance countered with a question of his own.

"Yep. All done."

"Get them to check all the fences to make sure no limbs fell on them in the rainstorm."

"Will do. Where are you? Are you still dealing with that wreck?"

"Yeah," he said, and clicked off before Monty could get in another question.

Chance hurried for the stairs to get dressed. On the third step he stopped. Was he seeing things? Was there a light coming from Judd's study?

He eased down the stairs and went to check, thinking it might be the early morning sun reflecting off the big front windows. He walked into the hall. The doors to Judd's study were closed and there was definitely a faint light coming from within—a light that hadn't been there earlier. Was Renee up and looking for something? But the study was Judd's private sanctum and it wasn't like his mother to be up this early.

Slowly, Chance opened one of the French doors, and received the shock of his life. Shay had Judd's safe open and was rummaging through it. What the hell?

She closed the safe and turned the knob. Then she saw him. In the light of the lamp on the desk he could see the blood drain from her face.

Chance glanced from her to the safe and then back to her startled eyes. "What are you doing in here?"

"Nothing." She edged around the desk.

"You had the safe open. What were you looking for?"

"Nothing." She moved farther away and held out her hands, palms up. "I didn't take anything."

"Come on. Who are you? What are you doing here and how did you know the combination to the safe?"

Before he guessed her intentions, she darted past him, ran through the foyer and slammed the front door in his face. He immediately ran after her, only to see her jump into the rental and tear out of the driveway.

Since he didn't have his boots on and his truck was at the bunkhouse, Chance didn't even try to follow. It was too late; she was already long gone.

He cursed himself while dressing. Walker had her address, and Chance was going to track down Shay Dumont if it was the last thing he did.

In a matter of minutes he had her Houston address from Walker. Chance told him about the incident, and the constable wanted to put an All Points Bulletin out on her. Chance kept seeing the fear in Shay's eyes, however, and wanted to find out firsthand what she was after. The law officer reluctantly agreed, but they both knew Judd was going to be pissed. It was up to Chance to make everything right. He felt he owed that to Judd for bringing her into the house.

He didn't tell Renee much—only that the rental had been delivered and their mysterious guest had left. The older woman was disappointed.

He checked on the cowboys and put Monty in charge. Then, after filling his truck with gas, Chance headed for Houston.

Thanks to the GPS in his truck, her house was easy to find. He took the Airline Drive exit from the freeway. She lived in the north central area of Houston, in an older neighborhood. He pulled up near a small, cream-colored frame house with brown shutters. The paint was peeling and the place needed a good coat of fresh color.

A bright blue house was next door, the two set closer than the others on the block. The yard was hard to miss, since about a dozen pink flamingoes stood among plastic windmills, birdhouses and birdbaths. On the garage door was a sign: Nettie's Beauty Nook. Evidently the garage had been converted into a beauty shop.

Shay had said something about a cousin who helped her. That could be her house.

Farther down the street two guys were working on a car, with a stereo blasting. Cigarettes dangled from their lips and tattoos ran up their arms. Another car sat to the side with grass growing around it. Chance had a feeling the neighborhood wasn't too safe.

He turned into Shay's driveway and parked. Time to meet her and her family. Climbing from the truck he strolled up the walk. There wasn't a bell so he knocked.

No one came to the door, but he could hear voices inside. Suddenly the door opened a crack, the safety chain still attached.

"What do you want?" a girl about seven or eight asked. In jeans, sneakers and T-shirt, she seemed overly thin. Her brown hair was cut short like a boy's, and she wore wire-rimmed glasses that were so lopsided he wondered how she saw anything out of them.

"You better close the door," a boy about the same age said from behind her. "Your mom said we weren't supposed to open it to strangers."

Mom? Shay had a kid?

The girl spared the boy a sharp glance. "You're such a scaredy-cat."

"Am not." He peered around her shoulder to the driveway. "Look, Darce, he's got a truck."

She followed his gaze and then looked at Chance. "Does it have a Hemi?"

Chance was taken aback by the question. Most kids her age wouldn't know the term. "Do you know what a Hemi is?"

"Yes." She nodded and straightened her glasses. "It's a tough truck that will go through mud, creeks and mountains. It can do anything." She pointed to the boy. "His brother is saving up for one and has pictures all over his wall."

"I see." Chance had to smile at the imagination of children. He glanced over his shoulder. "My truck is a Chevy four by four."

"Then it's a piece of junk." The girl had a razor-sharp tongue and the attitude of a cowboy who'd had too many beers the night before.

He couldn't stop thinking that this was Shay's child, and that Shay probably had a husband as well. She had a family and was trying to rob the Calhouns. That didn't fit. She was too nice.

Whoa, cowboy. He was letting his heart rule his head because he was smitten with her. Feeling that way about a woman hadn't happened in a long time. And it felt good. But now he had to think with his head.

"Go away," the girl said, and made to slam the door. But he put his booted foot in the opening, that had become wider as they were talking.

"I'd like to talk to Shay, please," he said politely.

"Sic him, Tiny," she said to the dog fussing around her feet.

The small canine, a cross between a Chihuahua and something else, launched himself through the crack. Latching on to Chance's jeans with his sharp teeth, Tiny shook his head as if he were a Doberman about to take down a rottweiler.

Chance reached down and dislodged the dog from his jeans. He rubbed the animal's head, and Tiny growled deep in his throat. "Think I'll take you home with me. I know two little boys who'll give you a run for your money." Chance had no plans to take the dog.

He just wanted to get the girl's attention. And he did.

"Hey. You can't do that. That's my dog." She quickly undid the safety chain and charged outside.

"Maybe little girls who are rude shouldn't have a dog."

"Darcy, where are you?"

"Uh-oh," the little boy said.

"I'm at the front door."

"What are you…" Shay's voice trailed away when she saw Chance, and her eyes were huge. Evidently she'd thought he wouldn't follow her.

"This man wanted to see you and I wouldn't let him in."

"You're not supposed to open the door to strangers. Period."

"I'm eight years old. I'm not a baby."

"Darcy, don't talk back to me."

Shay was still reeling from the shock of seeing Chance Hardin, and now she was arguing with her adopted daughter in front of him. What did he want? Well, that was a no-brainer; after the way she'd left Southern Cross.

She'd trembled all the way home, listening for the sound of a siren. She'd thought she was home free, but he'd followed her. Damn. What should she do now?

"Shay, where in the hell are you?"

Darcy frowned. "The witch's been calling for you."

"Do not call Blanche a witch." Shay's nerves were about to snap. She couldn't deal with Chance, her mother and Darcy all at the same time. At the moment he was the most pressing problem. Chance was glaring at her with those beautiful dark eyes, and she almost forgot she had to get rid of him.

"Mother, I'll be there in a minute."

"You finally dragged your ass home. That kid is making too much noise."

Shay cringed that Chance was listening to this.

"I was at the shop," she called back. "Just give me a few minutes, please."

"I want a glass of iced tea."

"Fine. I'll fix it."

Shay turned to her daughter. "Go outside and play with Petey, and we'll talk later."

Darcy jerked her thumb toward Chance. "He has Tiny."

Shay wondered about that. What was he doing with Darcy's dog? And how could she get Tiny back without causing a scene? Before she could form a plan, Chance placed Tiny on the concrete and he trotted to Darcy. She lifted the dog in her arms, hugging him as he whimpered, and then she and Petey ran outside.

Now Shay had to talk to Chance. She felt like running outside, too. But she steeled herself and faced him. *This is what you get,* she thought, *when you try to rob houses—a harsh dose of reality.*

"You left in rather a hurry, didn't you?" One eyebrow lifted beneath his Stetson. She ignored the hammering of her pulse.

"How did you get my address?"

"The constable looked up your license plate. High Cotton might be a small town, but we're not idiots."

She bit her lip. "What do you want?"

His eyes met hers in a direct, no-nonsense stare. "The truth, Shay *Dumont.* The honest-to-God truth." He dragged out her name as if to remind her of her lie.

She tucked her hair behind her ears. "Okay, I lied. My real name is Shay Dumont."

"Why?" His voice was as cool as ice water, and she trembled. But it didn't keep her from noticing how good-looking he was. Tall and lean, with everything a girl could want in between. How she wished they had met before she'd pulled such a stupid stunt.

She swallowed and wasn't sure what to say to him. The truth would hurt too many people. "Listen. I didn't take anything from Southern Cross, so can we please let this drop?"

"No."

She should have known that he didn't plan to be lenient. He'd come for the truth and he wasn't leaving without it. *The truth.* It was a can of worms that had been festering for over twenty years, and once opened, it would stink from Houston to High Cotton. How could she open that can? She had to stall, or maybe entice the handsome cowboy. She stopped herself from laughing out loud at the ridiculous thought. What did she know about enticing?

Chance shoved his hands into the front pockets of his jeans. "Let me make this easy for you." He could see she was thinking of dancing around the truth. He had to apply pressure. "If you don't tell me why you were trying to rob the Calhouns, I'll call the constable of High Cotton. He'll notify the police here and they'll arrest you for attempted robbery and take you back to High Cotton to face the charges." He gave her a second to digest that. "Do you want to put Darcy through that?"

Shay paled. "You wouldn't."

"You know I would. I wouldn't have come here otherwise."

She winced. "I thought you were nice, but you're not."

"I'm the foreman of Southern Cross and re-sponsible for everything that happens while the Calhouns are away."

"I didn't take anything, okay?" Her voice grew angry.

"I don't know that for sure. When I came in, you had the safe open and were rummag-ing through it. What were you after? And how did you get the combination?"

Her head jerked up. "You saw me leave, and could see that I didn't take anything. How many times do I have to say that?"

"But you were after something. I just in-terrupted you."

Shay gazed down at her sneakers and re-mained silent.

The shattered look on her face twisted his stomach and prompted him to add, "Shay, I mean you no harm, but I have to know why you tried to rob Southern Cross—a house in a small out-of-the-way town."

She still remained silent.

"If you're innocent, I'll forget the whole thing."

Her hands curled into fists. "But I'm not innocent." The words came out low, but he heard them.

He felt a blow to his chest. For the first time he realized he wanted her to be innocent, or to have a very good explanation. In a short amount of time she'd awakened his heart. He'd thought it had stopped working long ago, but one look into her green eyes had started him thinking of happy endings and the fairy tales his mother used to read to him.

Shay looked him in the eye. "If I tell you the truth, will you promise I won't be arrested? I can't leave Darcy. I'm all she has." She sighed heavily. "And, yes, I should have thought of her before...."

"Why didn't you?" When he saw the kid, he'd wondered why she'd take such a risk. There had to be a reason. "Where is the child's father?"

"Darcy is my adopted daughter. Her parents are dead." Shay heaved another sigh. "I did a very stupid thing because—"

"Shay!" a woman's voice shouted, through a fit of coughing.

Shay glanced over her shoulder. "I really have to go."

Chance placed his hand on the door to keep her from closing it. "Not until you tell me."

They stared at each other, one unyielding, the other determined. Shay knew she was beaten and had no choice. She had to open that can and reveal secrets that should never be told, at least to her way of thinking. It was a little late to realize her foolishness, but she had to consider Darcy now. First, though, she had to have some assurance.

"Promise I won't be arrested."

"If you didn't take anything, I'll do all I can to get Judd to drop the whole thing."

She frowned. "Why do you have to tell him?" She didn't want anything to do with the Calhouns. Her momentary-insanity jaunt had made her realize she didn't belong at Southern Cross. She should have kept that door closed, as always.

"Because he's the owner of Southern Cross, and as his foreman I don't keep things from him."

"Do you have the word *loyalty* tattooed across your butt?" The question slipped out before she could stop it.

His lips twitched into a grin. "Yes."

Shay realized the conversation had switched into flirtation. This could be easy.

She flipped back her hair. "Maybe you'll show me one day."

"Maybe," he drawled, and then his voice became serious again. "But first you have something to tell me."

Damn. She should have known this wouldn't be easy. He probably really *did* have *loyalty* tattooed on his butt.

"Well?" He waited.

She tried to speak, but her tongue seemed glued to the roof of her mouth.

"Shay."

Her name sounded so wonderful on his lips. It reminded her of lovers, moonlight and... What was she thinking? There was never going to be anything between her and Chance Hardin, especially after she told him the truth, and for a number of other reasons.

The words hovered in her throat and then she blurted them out. "My mother was once married to Jack Calhoun."

Chance felt as if he'd been kicked in the head by the meanest bronc in Texas. Had he heard her correctly? "Excuse me?"

"My mother, Blanche Dumont, was Jack's second wife. He lavished her with jewels and anything she wanted, but in the end he took everything from her, including her wedding rings." Shay drew a long breath. "As I told you, my mother is dying of lung cancer and she's obsessed with Jack Calhoun. He's all she thinks about. She's been pressing me for months about her rings. She wants to be buried with them on her finger, so she devised this plan.... That's what I was doing in High Cotton." Shay grimaced. "But things went awry."

The name finally clicked. Blanche Dumont—the stepmother from hell. How many times had he heard Judd say that? But not lately. Since Judd and Cait had found happiness, Blanche's name was no longer mentioned. Judd had filed that away under his father's bad taste in women.

Chance barely remembered the details. He'd been just a kid, but everyone in High Cotton knew of Jack Calhoun's love triangle with Renee and Blanche.

"How...how were you planning on getting in the house? You didn't..."

"Have the wreck on purpose?" she finished for him. "I may have been under pressure, but I'm not that stupid. I didn't plan on being gone overnight, either. I would never leave Darcy that long."

Chance was glad to hear that, but he was still grappling with the truth. Could Shay be Judd's half sister? How old was she? And how did you ask a woman that question?

"I was distracted with my phone," she was saying. "I was going to introduce myself as Blanche's daughter and ask for the rings, or demand them, as my mother wanted me to."

"The asking part would have worked. The Calhouns are very nice people."

"My mother didn't have a good relationship with Renee, and I wasn't sure." Shay shrugged. "It doesn't matter now. Once I met her I couldn't do it. She was too kind. But…" Shay hesitated. "When I left you in the kitchen, I had a wild idea to check and see if the rings were still in the safe, as my mother had said. The moment I saw the jewelry in the velvet box I knew it would be robbery. Just because something once belonged to you doesn't mean it still does. I couldn't take the rings—not even for my mother."

Chance's eyes narrowed. "How did you get the combination?"

"From my mother. She got it out of Jack

one night when he was drunk. I was surprised it still worked."

"Nothing much ever happens in High Cotton. It would take a real crazy person to come onto a ranch that size with armed cowboys everywhere."

She held up a hand. "That would be me."

Her green eyes sparkled and he had to resist that lure. "Why didn't Blanche ask for the rings after Jack's death?"

"She would never belittle herself to Renee."

"But she'd ask her daughter to steal?"

Shay stepped back, her hand on the door. "You got what you wanted, now, please leave."

Silence stretched as they stared at one another. He had so many things to say, questions to ask, but all he could do was stare into her eyes and wish there was such a thing as a happy ending instead of pain and heartache.

"I'm sorry if my coming here has hurt you and—"

"Just keep your promise," she replied, and closed the door.

Chance's step was a little slower as he walked to his truck. *Blanche Dumont.* He didn't know that much about her, and what he'd heard wasn't good. Rumor was that Blanche had enticed Jack away from Renee with lies. The two women used to be friends, waitresses together, but that all ended when Jack walked into their lives. They then became enemies fighting for the man's attention. It was a weird love triangle, and now there was Shay. Blanche's child—a daughter no one knew about.

As Chance reached his truck, he saw two kids inside—Darcy and Petey. Darcy was in the driver's seat, pretending to turn the wheel.

Chance opened the door. "What are you two doing?"

His voice must have come out rough, because Darcy seemed to shrink away from him. But her stubborn chin told him she wasn't afraid. "Driving your truck to see if it's a piece of junk," she retorted.

"You should have asked permission first."

"Uh-oh, there's Mom. We gotta go." The girl crawled out of the truck, followed by her friend, and ran to Shay, who was standing at the backyard gate.

Chance and Shay's eyes met for a brief second as he slid into his truck. He remembered a line from a movie: "You can't handle the truth." Maybe it was best if he forgot the

whole thing for his friends', the Calhouns',
sake. The truth would be a blow to all of them.

But what about Shay?

Chapter Three

The trio walked into the house in silence. Darcy and Petey hurriedly sat at the kitchen table and buried their heads in their homework. Shay glanced at her watch.

"Petey, it's time for you to go home. Your mom should be off by now. She only works until noon on Saturday. I'll phone to make sure."

Petey gathered his books and Shay placed the call. Sally was divorced, working two jobs to make a living. Petey was usually at their house unless his teenage sister or brother watched him. It was a sad situation, but Shay's was no better. She sighed. Between

Darcy and her mother she had no life. But she never regretted for a minute honoring Beth's wishes concerning Darcy. Shay just wished she knew how to handle her and how to handle her mother. She wished for a lot of things, and at the top of the list was a dark-eyed cowboy who took her breath away. A cowboy she would never see again.

"Shay?"

"She's calling again," Darcy remarked, writing in a workbook.

"I can hear," Shay replied. "Stay put and finish your homework."

"Yes, ma'am," the girl muttered.

"Shay!"

She ran to her mother's room. Blanche sat up in bed, propped on pillows, with tubing in her nose hooked to an oxygen machine on the floor. Her blond hair was now white. Nettie used to bleach it, but Blanche couldn't stand the fumes anymore. She'd been a beautiful woman with blond hair, green eyes and a svelte figure. A lot of people said Shay looked like her. Shay hoped that was all she'd inherited from her mother.

As hard as she had tried, she couldn't get the cigarette smell out of the room. Her mother had been a chronic smoker.

"What took so long?" Blanche asked, through another fit of coughing.

"It wasn't that long." Shay fluffed up her pillows.

"You were busy with that kid. How… many…times…do I—"

"And how many times do I have to tell you Darcy is here for good? She's been with me for four years and is legally my daughter. Why can't you understand that?" Shay didn't know why she even asked the question. Her mother was very jealous and resented the time Shay spent with Darcy.

"Who was at the front door earlier?"

"Just someone wanting directions," Shay said, hoping to keep the Calhouns out of the conversation.

"Don't lie to me," Blanche snapped.

Shay resisted the urge to bite her nails. "Okay. It was Chance Hardin."

Her mother sat up. "From the Southern Cross?"

"The one and only."

"Why didn't you invite him in?"

"He was here to have me arrested if I didn't tell him why I was looking through the safe. That's not someone I want to invite in."

"But don't you see he could be our way to get my rings?"

Our way? "Excuse me?"

"If you fixed yourself up, you could look halfway decent."

"Thank you," Shay said through clenched teeth, while straightening the bed, that was littered with glamour magazines.

"Don't you see a woman can make a man do anything she wants?"

"I must have missed that class in school." But she'd certainly learned it from her mother. Maybe that's why Shay was still single.

Blanche leaned back, her eyes narrowed. "You're a pitiful excuse for a daughter and for a woman."

"Yes, you've told me that before."

"If I had been like you, I would never have gotten Jack. But I went after him with every trick in a woman's arsenal and I got him… until he met that bitch again."

Shay held up a hand. "I'm not listening to the Jack, Renee and Blanche story again. I've heard it a thousand times. And for the record, I'm not ever going back to Southern Cross. The past is the past and we both have to accept that."

"Get out of my room, you no-good daughter!" Blanche screeched, and dissolved into a bout of coughing.

Shay waited until she stopped, and then walked out. This type of environment wasn't good for Darcy, but they had few options.

What a life.

"Shay," her mother called, before she could make it to the kitchen. Shay sucked in a patient breath and went back.

"What?"

"Did you tell Mr. Hardin why you were there and who you are?"

Oh, God, her mom never listened or let up. "Yes."

Blanche rubbed her hands in glee. "We should be hearing from the mighty Calhouns then."

"If we hear from them, it will be to have me arrested."

"Oh, silly, don't you see we have them over a barrel? You're Jack Calhoun's daughter and we're going to get what's coming to us."

"I didn't tell him I was Jack's daughter. Only that you were my mother."

"Well, that was stupid."

"Don't you understand I broke into their safe? They could have me arrested."

"You were so close. I don't know why you

didn't just grab them. You've let me down once again."

Shay shook her head and walked out again before she screamed. There was no talking to Blanche in this mood. There was no talking to her in any mood. When Blanche became so verbally abusive, Nettie had suggested that Shay put her in a nursing home. But there was a bond between mothers and daughters, and no matter how bruised, battered or bent, the tie was still there. Shay couldn't do it in the last stages of her mother's life. That would be cruel.

Even though Blanche had been embittered by the divorce and Jack's rejection, she'd lived life to the fullest. In her later years that bitterness had turned to hatred—not at Jack, but Renee. Blanche held Jack on a pedestal, and Shay didn't understand that. She didn't understand a lot of the past, because she looked at it through her mother's rearview mirror. Most of it had been glossed over to Blanche's benefit.

While at Southern Cross Shay could have told Renee several times who she was, but she hadn't. Instead, she'd lied. Somehow she'd sensed that Renee would be hurt, and Shay couldn't do it.

Over the years she'd often wondered why her mother had never told Jack or Renee about her. When she'd asked, Blanche had said that if Jack knew, he'd take Shay from her. He was supposedly that powerful. He'd once taken Judd from Renee, in fact. So Shay never broached the subject again. But there was a tiny worry in her head—why hadn't Blanche told Renee after Jack's death?

Soon the Calhouns would know about her. Shay was positive Chance would tell them. What would their next move be? Could Chance keep them from having her arrested? She really liked the cowboy. When he looked at her with those dark eyes, she felt as if she were floating in warm chocolate. She'd never felt such a strong sexual attraction before and it was an exhilarating feeling.

Entice him?

Her mother would explode if she knew Shay had tried and it hadn't worked. Chance would protect the Calhouns to the bitter end. His loyalty was with them. Not her.

When Chance got back to the Southern Cross, he explained Shay's situation to Walker. They agreed to wait for Judd's decision. Chance didn't tell Renee what he'd found out. He felt Judd needed to be there before he did.

On Monday Renee went in to Austin to shop, and Chance was glad. Judd and Cait should be home soon, and he'd tell them about Shay.

A part of him wanted to keep her secret, but the one he was already keeping was eating him up, and he wasn't doing that any more. Not even for a woman he couldn't stop thinking about. If she was Jack's daughter, why hadn't Blanche told Jack about her? A lot of the story didn't make sense. But he knew one thing: he was caught smack-dab in the middle.

He saddled up and headed out to check the Brahman cows that were about to calf. They kept records on each cow and calf, and had to know when a calf hit the ground. The cows looked good, knee deep in early coastal, but there were no new births. They had a tendency to all give birth around the same time. Then it was rodeo time as the cowboys branded and tagged each calf.

Chance rode back to the barn and dismounted. "Felipe, rub Chief down for me."

"Yes, sir." Felipe led the horse away.

As Chance reached the office, Brenda Sue,

Judd's secretary, came out. "Do you know when Judd is coming back?" she asked. "I have all these messages and I don't know what to tell people anymore. Looks like Judd could have left a date so I could tell people, but oh no, they just take off and—"

Chance held up a hand to stop her. If he didn't, she'd ramble on. "I don't know when he's coming back. Just take the messages. Okay?"

"Okay," she replied, and muttered "men" under her breath as she stomped off.

Removing his hat, Chance swiped a hand through his hair. He'd rather deal with an ornery bull than Brenda Sue. He heard the sound of a car and turned to see Cait's Escalade roll into the garage. They were home.

Chance went into the office, but couldn't concentrate. He wanted to give Judd and Cait time to settle in before he hit them with the news. After several minutes, he couldn't wait any longer. He strolled toward the house.

Cait, with one-year-old Justin in her arms, hugged him at the back door and invited him in.

"How was the trip?" he asked.

"Wonderful," she exclaimed, wiping Justin's mouth. The toddler was eating a cookie, with crumbs and saliva running down his chin.

Renee walked in holding Eli, a replica of Judd. Justin looked more like his mother.

"Look, Chance, my babies are home."

"I see."

"Okay, boys," Cait said. "Time for a nap."

"I'll put them down," her mother-in-law offered, and gathered Justin into her other arm. As she did, Judd came into the kitchen.

"Hey, Chance," he said in his booming voice. Judd was a big man with an even bigger presence. He was very much like his father, but Chance would never tell him that. Judd and Jack hadn't had a good relationship.

Chance had had a good relationship with his own father until…

"Do you have a minute?" He couldn't think about his parents. He had other things to handle.

"Sure. Let's go to my study."

Chance looked at Cait, who was nibbling on a cookie. "This concerns you, too."

"Oh, I'm honored I get to attend the pow-wow." Cait had black hair and the Belle blue eyes. She was a natural beauty, but Chance knew she could match any man in mental strength—even Judd.

"Don't be funny." Her husband slipped an arm around her waist. It was evident how much they loved each other. Chance hoped one day to find an everlasting love like that.

Cait kissed Judd's cheek and they walked down the hall to his study. Judd sat at his big mahogany desk and Chance and Cait settled in the burgundy wingback chairs. There were family photos on the desk, along with a sculpture of a magnificent horse. Pictures of prize Brahman bulls and thoroughbred horses hung on the walls.

"Is everything okay on the ranch?" Judd asked.

"Yes. Everything is running smoothly," Chance replied.

"Well, what has you looking like an old hound dog that's been beat a few times?"

Chance removed his hat and placed it on the arm of the chair. "There was an incident here at the ranch I thought you should know about." He told them about the accident and Shay.

"Damn it! She had the combination to my safe?" Judd jumped up, pulled back the picture and opened the safe. He searched through it. "There doesn't seem to be anything missing. What was she after?"

Chance took a breath. "The jewelry, or more precisely the wedding rings."

Judd frowned. "What the hell are you talking about? What jewelry? What rings?"

Chance hesitated, hating to shatter Judd's world.

"Come on, Chance. What are you dancing around, but not saying?"

"Shay wanted her mother's wedding rings."

Judd's frown deepened. "Who's her mother and what would her rings be doing here?"

Chance swallowed and said, "Blanche Dumont."

"What?" The rancher visibly paled.

Chance rushed into speech to ease his friend's confusion. "When Shay gave a false name and left in a hurry, I felt I should find out who she really was and why she was rummaging through the safe. I found out more than I wanted. Blanche is dying of lung cancer and she wants to be buried with the rings your father gave her. She pressured Shay into coming here. Evidently your father gave Blanche the combination one time when he was drunk."

"I knew I should have changed it, but no one ever knew it but Dad and me." Judd reached into the safe and pulled out a black velvet box. Placing it on the desk, he said, "Dad told me her jewelry was in the safe, but he never said what to do with it."

At Judd's forlorn tone, Cait got up and went to his side. After rubbing his arm, she reached down and opened the box. Glistening jewels sparkled up at them.

Cait opened a small velvet box that rested among the other pieces. She gasped when she saw the diamond-studded wedding and engagement rings. "Wow, your dad was very generous."

Judd sat down with a thud. "A thought just crossed my mind. I hope I'm wrong, but how old is this Shay?"

"Probably somewhere in her late twenties," Chance replied. "I'm not sure, but Walker has a copy of her driver's license. He'd know."

Judd reached for his cell and pushed a button. He spoke to Walker and then hung up. "He's on a call. As soon as he gets back to his office he'll check."

"You're thinking she might be Jack's daughter?" Cait asked.

"It's a possibility, if she's in her late twenties." Judd drummed his fingers on the desk. "I don't want Mom to know anything about this until I can get it sorted out."

"What don't you want Mom to know?" Renée asked, appearing in the doorway.

Judd was immediately on his feet. "Don't worry. I'll take care of it."

"Don't be silly. I'm not a child." Before he could stop her, she walked into the room, her eyes on the jewelry.

"Are the boys asleep?" Cait asked, and Chance knew she was trying to distract her.

"What?" Renée was clearly distracted, but not by Cait. "Oh, yes, down like little angels." Her eyes never left the jewelry. "Judd, I know you love Cait, but isn't that a bit extravagant? Cait's not much of a jewelry person."

His sigh seemed to come from deep in his chest, as if he'd accepted the inevitable. He had to tell his mother the truth.

"They're not for Cait," he answered. "They belong to someone else."

"Who for heaven's sake?"

Judd looked at Chance for help.

"Renée," he said. "Remember that young woman who had the accident?"

"Sure, she was a lovely young thing. A pity she left so quickly."

"I went to Houston to find out why she left like that. When Walker ran a check on the license plate, he found it was registered to someone else—not 'Shay Stevens.' She lied about her name. That's why I was leery."

"Did you find out her real name?"

"Yes." He paused. "It's Shay Dumont."

Renee's eyes narrowed. "Is she any kin to Blanche Dumont?"

This time Chance looked at Judd, and Judd nodded. "She's Blanche's daughter."

"What?" The color drained from Renee's face. "Did…did Blanche send her here?"

"Yes," Chance replied, then told her the story about the rings and Blanche's health.

"So this jewelry—" Renee flung a hand toward the box "—belongs to Blanche. Jewelry that Jack gave her but then took back. Jewelry he likely got out and mooned over every once in a while. Jewelry he said he'd gotten rid of. That bastard!"

"Mom, Dad probably kept it because he didn't want Blanche to have it."

"Oh, dear son, you do not know your father." His mom reached across the desk and picked up the box and the rings. "That bitch will not see one piece of this jewelry. I'll make sure of that. How could he?" Tears welled in her eyes as she ran from the room.

"Mom," Judd called, but Renee didn't stop. He threw up his hands. "What a homecoming."

Cait gave him a nudge. "Go to your mother."

"I don't know what to say to her. I'll let her calm down first." Judd did not have a good relationship with his mother, either. When he'd been five, his dad had divorced Renee and paid off enough people to make sure he got custody. Judd had thought his mother just left him, and Jack never told him differently until he married Renee the second time. By then the mother-son relationship was strained. But then Cait came into Judd's life and everything changed. He forgave his mother and a new relationship began. At times, though, the past intruded. Cait was always the peacemaker.

"Say you love her. Jack loved her and the jewels mean nothing."

"Cait…"

"Do you mind if I talk to her?" Chance asked. He didn't know what to say to her, either, but decided to wing it. After all, he felt most of what had happened was his fault for bringing Shay here.

"No," Judd answered quickly. "But when she's angry, she's hell to deal with."

Chance took the stairs two at a time and knocked on Renee's door. She yanked it open. "Don't… Oh, Chance." Clearly, she was expecting Judd.

Chance had never been inside Renee's room before and it was a bit of a shock. Everything was pink and white, with ruffles and lace. Even the rug was white. He felt as if he was in Barbie land, and glanced down to make sure there was no mud on his boots.

Most of the jewelry was scattered across the bed, but the rings were in Renee's hand.

"Judd chickened out, huh?" she asked.

Chance didn't respond, and she added, "He's so much like Jack, who could never handle deep, true emotions. Thank God Judd has Cait."

"Yeah. He got lucky," Chance agreed.

"Cait doesn't take anything from Judd. She stands up to him and demands that he treat her as an equal, and he does." Renee shook her head. "I let Jack walk all over me in our first marriage, but I demanded some respect in our second. I thought he'd changed but—" she glanced toward the bed "—he kept *her* jewelry."

"I'm sorry you're hurt," Chance muttered.

"Hurt?" she screeched. "I'm not hurt. I'm damn angry."

Chance had to dig deep to find the right words. "Jack loved you. You were his one true love."

"Humph. Me and about thirty other women."

Now Chance knew why Judd didn't want to do this. Women loved to wring every last emotion out of a man. Jack had had only one feeling toward women—lust. And like other men, Chance didn't want to broach that subject.

He stepped closer. "Don't you think you've won? You're here, living a pretty good life. She's not. She's dying of lung cancer and lives in a run-down neighborhood. The only thing she wants now is her wedding rings."

Renee's expression turned bitter. "She will never get them."

"You're not that cruel." Chance spoke before he thought. He wasn't taking Blanche's side; he just felt a dying person should have her last wish granted. The feeling came out of nowhere and it surprised him.

"You don't know me."

He looked straight at Renee. "Oh, but I do. I've seen you with the twins and Judd and Cait. I helped you catch a stray cat and hungry dog so you could feed them. Remember that old goat that appeared out of nowhere, and you fed it until the owner showed up?"

A slight smile touched her lips. "That goat

got up on Judd's new truck and caved in the top. Oh, he was mad."

There was silence for a moment and the bitterness seemed to tiptoe out the door.

"You have a happy life," Chance said. "She doesn't. Don't forget that."

Renee touched his cheek. "You're such a nice young man. You should be married with kids."

He frowned. "On that note, I'll leave." At the door he added, "I'm sorry you're hurt."

"Thank you. We should never have let that young woman in the house."

"But you liked her."

Renee lifted an eyebrow. "So did you."

He nodded and walked out. There was nothing left to say.

Chapter Four

Chance went down the stairs thinking that at thirty-four he should be married. Suddenly, all he could see was green eyes. He shook his head. There was no future there.

He walked back to the study, then stopped. Judd sat there with his face in his hands—an odd posture for such a strong man.

"Are you okay?" Chance asked, moving into the room.

His head jerked up. "How's Mom?"

"She's fine. Like you said, she just needs to cool off." Chance eyed his friend. "What's wrong?" From the look on Judd's face, he knew something was.

"I just heard from Walker."

"And?" Chance had a feeling the news wasn't good.

"She was born eight months after Blanche left here."

"So she could be Jack's daughter?"

"Yep."

"I'm sorry, Judd."

"Why?" he asked. "You didn't do anything. If you hadn't brought her to the house, she would have found another way to break into my safe. Our lives."

Chance waited a second. "What are you planning on doing about it?"

"Have the damn numbers changed."

"No, I mean about Shay."

Judd looked up. "I'm not sure yet. Why?"

"I'd liked to ask a favor." He'd promised Shay he would ask, and for some reason he felt she needed a break. The way her mother kept screaming at her had made him realize her life wasn't easy.

"What?"

"That you not report it or have Shay arrested. She has a little girl to raise, and she was pressured by her dying mother. Shay is caretaker for both, and I don't believe a woman like that should be in jail."

Judd leaned back, his hands behind his head. "One favor deserves another."

"What?" Chance couldn't imagine what Judd could want from him.

"That you get Shay Dumont to take a DNA test. I'll arrange it at a lab in Houston. Dad's DNA and mine are on record in Austin. After all the lies Blanche told Dad about Mom, he wanted to make sure I was his. Nice family background, huh?" Judd leaned forward, not waiting for an answer. "I want to be positive before this goes any further."

Chance hesitated and then said, "I'll give it my best shot, but I have a feeling she's going to resent being asked."

Judd picked up a pen. "Is that a problem for you?"

Chance silently met the rancher's knowing gaze.

"I'm getting a vibe that you like this woman."

"Yes, I like her. She's going through a rough time and has a young child to support."

"Is there a husband in the picture?"

"No, and the child is adopted. Shay seems like a very nice person with a lot of bad stuff going on in her life. I mean bad people don't adopt kids or take care of their dying mothers."

"You have the biggest heart of anyone I know," Judd murmured.

"You mean I'm a sucker for a sad story."

"No, I mean you take people at face value. I'm too much like Dad to trust anyone." Judd waved a hand. "It doesn't matter. Do we have a deal?"

Chance took a moment, wondering how he'd gotten into the middle of this. "Yes." He picked up his hat and studied it. "There's something else I'd like to talk about."

"Your brothers?"

Chance looked up. "How did you know that?"

"You've been restless since Cadde inherited that oil company. Because of your father, the oil business is your first love."

"Yeah." Chance felt an ache in his heart. Shay's situation made him realize keeping secrets could destroy people. He had to find a way to tell his brothers. "Cadde asked me to join him, but I like it here at Southern Cross."

"If you're worried about the ranch, Cait and I can handle it. Follow your dream, Chance. It only comes around once."

His dream… Was it still the same as it had been when he was a kid—to work with his brothers? The only thing holding him back was what he knew and Cadde and Cisco didn't. And, of course, his loyalty to Cait and Judd.

"I hate to leave at a time like this."

"Go, Chance. Cait and I want only what's best for you."

Chance placed his hat on his head. "Then I guess I'm formally resigning as foreman of Southern Cross."

They shook hands, and Chance hoped he didn't regret this sudden decision. He had felt the pull of his brothers ever since he'd talked to them at High Five. *The Hardin boys against the world.* They used to say that all the time. They'd first planned to be Texas Rangers, fighting for their home state. Then they'd decided to be firefighters, saving victims. But then the army sounded better. They'd fight for their country. Whatever they dreamed about, it always included a lot of fighting.

Their father would say his boys should get an education and not be roughnecks all their lives. That they would work their way up the ladder, learn the business and one day own an oil company. The best way to take on the world was with money, and there was a lot of money in the oil industry. And he would be there to help them every step of the way. But he wasn't.

* * *

A week later Chance had all his worldly belongings packed into a box and a suitcase. Not much to show for thirty-four years. The only thing he had of value was his truck, a share of his parents' home, which was rotting away, and a hefty bank balance, that would now go into Shilah Oil. Before leaving High Cotton he made a sizable donation to the volunteer fire department.

He said a sad goodbye to the Calhouns and the Belle sisters. Aunt Etta and Uncle Rufus said they wanted him to be happy, but Aunt Etta cried as he left. That wasn't easy.

As he neared Giddings he pulled over to the side of the county road and stared at the oak tree where his parents had died. Pieces of bark were missing where the car had hit it. One part of the tree was dead from the fire. Half dead, half alive. That's how he felt inside.

Chance and his brothers had thought their father could walk on water. It was heartbreaking to find out he couldn't. But only Chance knew that. It was time to tell Cadde and Cisco.

He said a silent goodbye and drove toward a new beginning, a new life.

In his right pocket was the address of a lab in Houston he had agreed to give Shay. Judd had called and arranged to have Jack's DNA records transferred there.

As Chance pulled into Shay's driveway, he saw four kids in the yard: Darcy, Petey and two other boys. Darcy had a baseball in her hand and she was holding it high, out of reach of the boy jumping for it.

Suddenly the boy pushed Darcy, and she threw the ball, hitting the kid in the chest. He fell to the ground moaning. The other boy then jumped on Darcy, punching her in the stomach, in the face, while Petey tried unsuccessfully to pull him off.

Chance leaped out of his truck and reached for the boy's collar, yanking him away. Out of the corner of his eye he saw Shay flying across the neighbor's yard. She sank down beside Darcy, who was now on the ground, her lip bleeding. Her glasses lay in the grass.

Shay tugged her blouse out of her jeans and used the end to wipe Darcy's mouth. Then she glanced at the boy Chance was still holding by the collar. "What have you done to her?"

Chance pulled the boy forward. "Tell her what you did."

"I hit her 'cause she hit my brother in the chest with the ball, and she's mean."

Shay helped Darcy to sit up. Petey retrieved her glasses and handed them over. "Why would she hit Michael in the chest?" Shay asked.

"Because he pushed her," Petey said. "Real hard."

"What was she doing with your baseball?"

Chance reached down and pulled the other boy to his feet. "Truth time, boys."

Before they could answer, an overweight woman in flip-flops and a housedress rushed over from the house next door. "What's going on? Why are you holding my boys?"

"They attacked a helpless girl."

"Darcy? Helpless?" The woman laughed.

Shay rose to her feet and faced the woman, pointing a finger in her face. "You say one more word about Darcy and I'll put your lights out, Velma. From now on keep your boys in your yard and I'll keep Darcy in ours. If they step one foot over the line, I'm calling the police."

"Don't be silly, Shay. My boys meant her no harm."

"Take a look at her lip. You call that no harm?" Fire lit up Shay's green eyes.

Chance thought he should intervene before she did put her neighbor's lights out. He tugged the boys forward. "Tell your mother what happened, and remember I saw the whole thing."

But Petey answered, "Their ball came into the yard. Darcy was going to give it back, but Bruce called her some ugly names and she wouldn't. They chased us to the front yard. Michael pushed Darcy and she threw the ball at him. Then Bruce jumped on her and hit her in the stomach and face."

"You hit a girl much smaller than you, didn't you," Chance said.

Bruce hung his head.

"Go to the house," Velma said to her sons.

"Not so fast, ma'am." Chance held tight to the boys. "If Bruce or Michael harm Darcy again in any way, I'm going to come calling. And it won't be friendly." He let go of the boys and they ran home, followed by their mother.

Shay picked up Darcy and went into the house. Chance and Petey walked behind her. He wasn't invited, but he went in anyway, wanting to make sure the little girl was okay. Closing the door, he glanced around. Worn carpet covered the floor and the furniture was old and shabby, but everything was clean and neat.

On the wall was a picture of a beautiful blonde holding a baby. It had to be Blanche and Shay. The adult Shay had a striking resemblance to her mother.

He walked to the sofa, where Shay had placed Darcy, and was now cleaning her wound. "It's going to be blue tomorrow. It's already swelling," she murmured.

"I could have taken 'em," Darcy muttered. "But he—" she pointed to Chance "—stopped 'em."

Shay was kneeling on the floor, and sank back on her heels. "No fighting. Period. We're going to have a long talk about this tonight. Very long."

"Oh, jeez." Darcy buried her face in the sofa.

"I gotta go," Petey said, and grabbed his backpack.

Shay pulled her cell phone out of her pocket and poked in a number. She seemed very careful to ignore Chance. "Nettie, could you please finish up for me? Okay, thanks. I'll talk to you later." She rose to her feet. "Mr. Hardin, what are you doing here?" The fire was still in her eyes, but now it was directed at him.

"To talk to you."

"As you can see, I'm very busy. Maybe you could come back later." *Or never,* Shay thought. Whatever he wanted to discuss had to do with the Calhouns, she was sure. And she wasn't in a mood for that.

"It's important," he said. "It won't take long."

He wasn't going to budge. She could see that by the strong thrust of his chin, so decided she might as well get it over with.

She glanced at Darcy. "Stay put. I'll get some ice for your lip."

"Okay," the girl muttered.

Shay turned to Chance. "I'll talk to you in the kitchen."

He settled down at the table without saying a word while she prepared the ice pack. His silence made her nervous as hell. She carried the ice to Darcy and found she was sound asleep. Pulling a cushion forward, she positioned the pack on it against the girl's lip.

Then Shay straightened her spine and went to speak to Mr. Hardin. She had to get him out of the house before Blanche heard him. That deep Texas drawl could wake an angel, so her mom must be in a deep sleep. Glancing toward the bedroom, Shay decided she had better check. She didn't want Chance and Blanche to meet. That could be dangerous.

Her mom was snoring away, so Shay hurried back to the kitchen and sank into a chair. "What is it, Mr. Hardin?"

"So friendly," he said, his dark eyes watching her.

She felt a shiver run through her. "We're not friends."

"Guess not." He leaned back in the old wooden chair and Shay thought how shabby the house must look to him. But she would not let him intimidate her. She was doing the best she could under very difficult circumstances. "It's sort of a good news, bad news sort of thing," he told her.

She blinked, losing her train of thought. "What?"

"Do you want the good or bad news first?"

"Don't play games, Mr. Hardin," she retorted.

"Judd agreed not to report the attempted robbery."

"Oh." Relief surged through her. "I appreciate that. But what's the other part?"

He pulled a piece of paper out of his pocket and pushed it toward her.

She glanced at it. "The address and phone number of a lab in Houston... What has that got to do with me?"

With his eyes on her face, he said, "Judd would like for you to take a DNA test."

Shay frowned. "Why?"

"To see if you're Jack's biological daughter. I'm sure you're aware of that possibility."

"It's not a possibility. It's a fact," she said. "I'm not asking anything from Judd, so I don't understand why he wants the test. Ever since I was a baby Mom has told me I was Jack's daughter. The first words I learned were *Jack Calhoun.* I guess because my mother said his name so much. There's no way Blanche would lie about that. Besides, she was living with him when I was conceived, Mr. Hardin. Believe me, I checked."

"Then you have nothing to worry about, and the truth will be on record. Judd is a fair man, and once he knows the truth, he'll probably want to make a financial settlement." Chance glanced around the kitchen. "I'm sure you could use the money."

"What?" Fire shot through her veins. "My

home's not good enough for you, Mr. Hardin?"

His eyes held hers and she trembled. "First, I live in a bunkhouse that just has the necessities of life. It's a place to sleep, eat and bathe. Second, would you please stop calling me Mr. Hardin?"

She felt about two feet tall and wanted to crawl under the table. "I didn't mean…"

"I know. I'm not a Calhoun. My name is Chance."

She knew that. "But you're a big part of the Southern Cross."

"Not anymore," he said. "I'm on my way into Houston to join my brothers in an oil venture."

So many questions ran through her head. "Did you and Judd get into an argument?"

"No. Judd's not like his father. He treats his employees with respect."

She clenched her hands together in her lap. "All I know about Jack is what my mom told me, and it's all good."

"No offense, but I think Blanche enjoyed the money and the life of luxury."

Shay couldn't help but smile. "She always did like the finer things."

Chance grinned back, and Shay wrapped

her arms around her waist to stop the pleasure flowing through her. He had an off-the-
Richter-scale smile.

"Take the test." He pushed the paper closer.
"It can only help you. And while you're in
Houston I'll take you out to lunch or dinner.
Your choice." He pulled a pen out of his shirt
pocket, reached for the paper and wrote his
number on the back. She noticed his strong
hands.

She took the sheet and met his gaze, wondering if that last part had just slipped out
before he'd thought about it. He was asking
her for a date, but she couldn't get involved
with Chance Hardin.

"Okay." She laid the paper in front of her.
"I'll take the test so everyone will know the
truth."

"Good," he said and got to his feet. Picking up his Stetson, he moved toward the front
door, his boots making a thudding sound on
the old linoleum. He stopped by the sofa and
stared down at Darcy. Tiny was now curled
up in her arms. "Those boys could have really hurt her."

"I know. I was just a couple seconds too
late. I had finished giving a lady a perm and
was taking her money when I saw them chase

Darcy and Petey to the front yard. Thank you for coming to the rescue."

Chance walked out the door and turned. "No problem. So you work at the beauty shop next door?"

"Yes." She smiled. "Would you like a manicure?"

"Thanks, but I'm not the manicure type."

"I knew that."

"How?"

"Cowboys don't get manicures."

"You got that right, except I had this cowboy friend who was getting married and he got a manicure and a pedicure. He wanted to make sure there was no dirt under his nails. They'd been dating for over a year. I told him if his gal hadn't seen dirt under his fingers and toes by now they were in big trouble."

Shay laughed out loud and realized she hadn't done so in a long time. She'd been under too much stress.

Smiling, he placed his hat on his head. "When I get married, I'll let you give me a manicure, but I don't like anyone messing with my feet."

On instinct she stepped closer. "And I promise to make it a pleasant experience." From the gleam in his eyes she knew they were talking about something else entirely and Shay hadn't been in those emotional waters for a very long time so she was treading lightly.

As his eyes darkened she forgot about lightly, forgot about not getting involved with him, and kissed his roughened cheek, breathing in his manly scent. "Thank you for helping Darcy, Chance."

Before she could move away, he cupped her face with his callused hands and kissed her lips softly. As his mouth moved over hers, it felt like the first sip of a martini, feeling the kick and wanting more.

"Mommy." Darcy's call effectively ended the kiss before it deepened.

"You better go," Chance said, rubbing her cheek with his thumb. Then he walked toward his truck.

She shivered, feeling deprived of something she wanted. Something she needed.

What was she doing? She couldn't get involved with him. But, oh, he was tempting.

Chapter Five

Chance had no problem finding Shilah Oil in downtown Houston. He'd been there before. The Murdock building was twelve stories high, with a huge sculpture of an oil derrick out front surrounded by flower beds.

He found a parking spot and got out. Glancing around at the crowded buildings, he experienced a moment of suffocation. He preferred wide-open spaces and fresh air. Sitting in an office all day wasn't for him. He liked the action of the actual drilling, and that's what he planned to do in his new job. He had to convince Cadde of that before he agreed to anything.

He walked into a large lobby with a marble floor. Above the round reception desk was a portrait of Roscoe and Alfred Murdock—brothers who'd started Shilah Oil in the 1940s. Al and his wife had passed on soon after the murder of their daughter, and Roscoe had become the sole owner. But when the oil business got rough, Roscoe took on investors who now sat on the board. He never made the company public, however. Shilah was Roscoe's own private empire, with a few friends who backed him.

Shilah meant brother in Navajo, and Chance thought that was very fitting for today—brothers working together.

Sofas, plants and chairs stood here and there. A pretty, green-eyed blonde sat at the reception desk. But they weren't the right green for him.

He still couldn't get that kiss out of his mind. Shay had felt and tasted just like he thought she would—all soft, sweet and enticing. Kissing her had short-circuited every other emotion in him. He wanted her, and she seemed to feel the same.

"May I help you?" Somewhere in his brain he heard the receptionist's sugarcoated words.

He quickly collected himself. "What floor

is Cadde Hardin on?" After Roscoe's death, Cadde had inherited a new office, and Chance wasn't sure exactly where. He hadn't told his brothers he was coming, so this was going to be a surprise.

The blonde smiled. "Do you have an appointment?"

"No."

She winked and he knew he was getting the come-on, but he wasn't interested. "I'll call his secretary and see if I can get you in," she told him, but as she picked up the phone he saw a directory on the wall. Cadde's name was at the top. Chance walked off to an elevator on the right.

"Hey, Mr.—" the receptionist called. The doors closed, cutting off whatever she was going to say.

Getting off the elevator moments later, Chance glanced around at the names on doors. Then he saw the large door at the end of the hall, with Cadde Hardin, CEO written boldly on it. He strolled in that direction. Opening the door, he walked into a secretary's office, but no one sat at the desk. She must be on an errand or something, he figured. Another door with Cadde's name on it was slightly ajar and he could hear Cadde and

Cisco. He could hear them very well, since they were yelling at each other.

"Stay away from the receptionist, Kid. She was in your office three times this morning. What does my receptionist have to do in your office?"

"That's none of your business."

Chance looked through the crack and saw Cadde at a big oak desk. Kid sat in the leather chair across from him, his booted feet propped on the desk. Cadde stood in an angry movement and knocked their brother's boots to the floor. Kid was instantly on his feet.

"Anything that concerns this company concerns me," Cadde yelled. He grabbed a large folder from his desk and slammed it down in front of Kid. "Has the Wilcox lease been signed? The Bradens'? The Carvers'? No. Because you've been fooling around with the receptionist. It ends now, Kid. I mean it."

"Now you're going to tell me who I can date?" Cisco took only so much before he exploded.

"If it concerns this company."

"God, all you ever think about is the company."

"You're damn right I do. I want this enterprise to succeed, not only for myself but for Dad's dream to come true."

Chance sagged against the wall. How could he tell them?

"So what's it going to be?" Cadde asked, sounding a little calmer.

Instead of answering, Kid said, "You're so wound up you're about to fly out of this room. Have you got a thing for the blonde?"

"I'm gonna break your damn neck," Cadde shouted, moving around the desk toward Kid.

Chance pushed open the door before a full-blown fight erupted. It reminded him of his childhood, always breaking up fights between Cadde and Kid. "Is this what I have to look forward to, working for Shilah Oil?"

Cadde swung around. "Chance!" The next minute he had him in a bear hug so tight he could barely breathe. Kid pulled Cadde away and hugged Chance in turn.

"Are you serious?" Cadde asked. "You're joining us?"

"Yep, or you two are going to kill each other."

Kid thrust a thumb toward Cadde. "It's him. Remember that old rooster Mom used to have? We could just step out of the house and he'd attack us, for no reason. Cadde re-

minds me of that rooster—always on the attack."

"Shut up, Kid." Cadde walked toward a
large map on the wall and motioned Chance
over. "We're drilling beneath the Austin
Chalk to tap into the Buda, Georgetown and
the Glen Rose formations. So far we've had
success in the Giddings field using horizon-
tal well technologies, which you're very fa-
miliar with."

"Yep. Busted my butt on a lot of those
wells."

"By drilling deeper we're having phenom-
enal results. The Eagle Ford shale beneath the
Austin Chalk is hell to get through, though.
That's why I want someone with your experience on the job." He tapped the map. "The
Rodessa field in northeast Texas extends
into Louisiana. Roscoe bought some of those
leases back in the 1960s. He never drilled in
Louisiana but kept renewing the leases. I'm
trying to get the board to approve a drilling site in Caddo Parish, but Jessie votes it
down every time and Roscoe's old cronies
vote with her."

A change came over Cadde's face, but in
an instant it was gone. He tapped the map
again. "The green dots are where we're drill-

ing now, the red dots leases that have been signed and are ready for drilling. The blue ones are leases we're trying to sign, but for some reason or another they haven't been." He glanced at Kid.

"Okay, okay," their brother said and headed for the door. "Glad to have you aboard, Chance."

"And get a damn haircut," Cadde yelled after him.

Before Kid could retaliate, Chance jumped in. "I need a place to stay until I can find an apartment. Can I bunk with one of you?"

Kid frowned. "I have a date tonight and she might want to stay over."

Cadde groaned. "Those leases had better be signed by tomorrow."

"Come on, Cadde."

Cadde pointed a finger at Kid. "Tomorrow." He walked to his desk. "With Jessie around it's about thirty degrees at my house."

"I wonder why," Kid murmured under his breath.

Cadde ignored him. "But you can stay at the Shilah Oil apartment." He threw Chance a pair of keys. "It's at the other end of the hall. Roscoe stayed in it, especially if he had a woman over."

"Thanks."

"So you're staying at the house tonight?" Kid couldn't leave well enough alone. "Don't you usually stay at the apartment?"

"Go to work, Kid."

Kid winked at Chance. "Must be a board meeting coming up. Cadde always tries to sweet-talk Jessie into voting his way. It never works. He can't sweet-talk a two-year-old."

"Go to work, Kid, or I *am* going to break your neck," Cadde responded.

Kid saluted and walked out.

Chance removed his hat and took a seat in one of the leather chairs in front of Cadde's desk. "What's my job?"

"Drilling operations. We have too many roustabouts who are fooling around and causing accidents. Last month two wells came in late because of silly incidents. I want those wells in on time." Cadde pointed upward. "There's a Shilah helicopter on the roof. We try to keep our two rigs going at all times, but sometimes they break down. That costs us time, and when the rigs are idle that costs Shilah money. I would like for you to visit each well every day and make sure things are on schedule, and they're following safety regulations. I want every worker to know that a boss is watching them."

"I can handle that," Chance said. "I was going to tell you that I'm not sitting at a desk all day. I like the outdoors."

"Well, brother, you'll be outdoors—a lot. Not on a horse, but in a helicopter. God bless Dane Belle. Who else would give teenage boys flying lessons? And God bless Aunt Etta and Uncle Ru for allowing Dane to indulge us." Cadde paused. "God, I miss him." There was a moment of silence, and then Cadde looked at him. "Have you kept your license up to date?"

Chance shifted in his seat. "Yeah. I fly once a month at the Giddings airport. I just never knew when I was going to use it for real." They seldom had a conversation that didn't include their father or Dane, and sometimes both. One was worthy, the other not, but Chance was the only one who knew that. Telling his brothers the truth was going to be the hardest thing he'd ever done, but he'd made up his mind.

Cadde pulled a piece of paper forward and wrote on it. "Shilah's warehouse where the rigs are worked on is out on US 290. Trucks and supplies are kept there, too. I'll give you a key."

"Okay." Chance leaned forward. "Let's talk about salary."

Cadde scribbled a number by the address. "You'll receive a monthly salary, a seat on the board and a percent of the profits at the end of each quarter. Sometimes there's a profit, sometimes not. Roscoe, not being in good health, made a lot of bad decisions in his last year. I'm trying to get everything back on track."

Chance reached for the paper and stared at the number. "This is higher than I expected."

"And it's going to get better," his brother boasted.

Chance reached into his pocket and pulled out a check. Placing it in front of Cadde, he asked, "Is that enough for my share?"

Cadde glanced at it. "Been saving those pennies, have you?"

"You bet. With free room and board there's not much to spend my wages on."

"Except a fancy truck."

Chance nodded. "Just one that does the job."

Cadde stood. "Let's go down the hall and I'll show you your office."

Chance looked around Cadde's big office, that had its own private elevator. One wall

was of glass, showcasing Houston and beyond. The floor was shiny hardwood, with
an Oriental rug in front of the desk. On the
wall behind was another portrait of Roscoe
and Al. Though it had been through its ups
and downs, the company was currently thriv-
ing. A lot of that had to do with Cadde.

Chance's heart stopped when he noticed
a framed photo sitting on an antique table:
Chuck Hardin and his three boys. Chance remembered the day it was taken. Cadde and
Kid's basketball team had just won the dis-
trict and were headed for the state championship—a week before the accident. A week
before their world was shattered.

Chance swallowed hard, pushing memories
away. "I hope it's not as lavish as this one."

"Nah. This is Roscoe's old office. He believed in spending his money. I saved one
down the hall just for you."

Chance placed his hat on his head and got
to his feet. "You were that sure I was coming?"

"Yep. You've heard about Dad's dream for
us most of your life, and I knew you wouldn't
forget that."

No, he never forgot his father—neither the
man he was nor the man he used to be.

* * *

The DNA test took only a few minutes.
They swabbed Shay's mouth, dropped the
swab in a glass tube and labeled it. The
girl told her she'd get the results within two
weeks. And that was it. Shay had left work at
four, thinking it would take longer.

She stood outside the lab, staring at Chance's
phone number. Should she or shouldn't she?
She wanted to but…

Getting into her rental car, she shoved the
paper back into her purse. It was the right
thing to do. Why didn't it feel right?

Backing out, she saw she had plenty of
time before her class at the University of
Houston. One day she'd get her degree so
she could make a better life for Darcy, but
finishing a degree in elementary education
was taking forever, since she could only take
night classes.

Instead of meeting Chance she drove to
the Galleria Mall and shopped, something
she rarely did. She found some jeans and a
T-shirt for Darcy on sale. That was Shay's
limit. She hated pinching pennies, but she
should be used to it. She'd done it all her life.

The whole time she was shopping she kept
glancing at her watch. She could be having

dinner with Chance, could be looking into those dark eyes. But she wasn't ready for a relationship, especially with a Hardin from High Cotton, Texas.

She stopped dead in the middle of the mall—so abruptly that a woman bumped into her, then gave her the evil eye. Shay ignored her and sank onto a bench. How could she tell Chance about her mother's many lovers? And that Blanche's number one goal had been to make it back to High Cotton and Jack Calhoun? She'd used many men to accomplish that, but it never happened. Blanche had caused only heartache and pain, and it was best for Shay not to get involved with anyone from that small community.

Basically, Shay was an honest person, and if she saw Chance she'd eventually have to tell him how vindictive her mother could be.

She reached in her purse for the number, intending to throw it in the trash. But for some reason she shoved it back inside once more.

Oh God! Was she going to be like her mother?

March turned into April and a lot of rainy days kept drilling to a minimum. That gave

Chance time to settle into the oil business and get acquainted with everyone.

Right away he called Aunt Etta, to let her know he was okay and adjusting. He made a mental note to phone every week to make sure they were all right. That was the only drawback about moving to Houston—he wouldn't be there to help them. One of the Belle sisters would call, though, if anything happened.

He traded his cowboy boots, Stetson and horse for a hard hat, steel-toed work boots and a helicopter. He'd forgotten how much he liked to fly. Roscoe's helicopter was a top-of-the-line Bell with all the trimmings. It was blue and white, with Shilah Oil written on each side. The man did like to spend money.

Chance flew to each well and introduced himself to the tool pusher and driller, the men in charge of the rig and workers, and then met some of the roustabouts and roughnecks. He couldn't meet them all, because they worked in eight-hour shifts seven days a week—night and day. After two weeks of work, they had a week off. By the end of his first week on the job, though, Chance had met just about everyone.

Taking over wasn't in his plan. That would

make everyone a little touchy. He always went to the tool pusher's trailer first, where the technical equipment was located. He checked the drilling log to see how many feet had been drilled, and to make sure the operation was on time. Through the small window he could see the workers on the rig, looking like tiny ants.

There were two mobile trailers on-site where the workers slept and ate. One well wasn't far out of Giddings, and sometimes when their shift ended they'd bathe and go into town to drink. Chance didn't like that and decided he'd have to talk to them. Nursing a hangover on a rig was too dangerous.

On his way back to Houston that day he looked at his phone to see if he'd gotten a call from Shay. He couldn't count the number of times he'd done that. Why hadn't she phoned? Had he misinterpreted the kiss? Was the emotion, the passion, all on his side? Or maybe she hadn't taken the test yet? Had she chickened out?

By the time he got back to his office, the lab was closed. First thing the next morning he called, and found Shay had taken the test last Tuesday—a week ago. That pretty much said it all.

He had to get Shay Dumont out of his mind. It had ended before it had even started. Besides, the situation between her and Judd was a sticky one. It was best for Chance to forget the whole thing. There was just something about her, though.

Cadde walked into his office not long after. "The Occupational Safety and Health Administration inspector will be here next Wednesday at eight o'clock, so show her around."

Chance looked up. "Isn't that your job?"

"No. It's yours." His brother walked out.

"Oh, no, it isn't." Chance followed him to his office.

Cadde sank into his chair. "It's a woman, and you handle women better than I do."

"Oh, good grief. Why don't you send Kid then?"

"No," Cadde snapped. "If she's younger than forty he'll make a pass at her and screw up the whole thing. This is serious because of the two accidents we've had."

"Okay, I'll do it. But I hope she doesn't have green eyes."

Cadde frowned. "What?"

"Nothing." Chance shook his head dismissively as Kid strolled in.

"What's going on?" Kid slid into a chair and propped his feet on Cadde's desk.

Chance told them about Shay and Blanche and their connection to the Calhouns. "So you see, I've kind of been the go-between."

"But you like this Shay despite what she did?" Cadde asked.

"Yeah," he replied. "It's hard to explain, though my first loyalty is to Cait and Judd."

"Hmm." Cadde was eyeing Kid's new haircut.

Their brother leaned back and placed his hands behind his head, causing the big chair to teeter on two legs. "Ol' Jack sure was a ladies' man."

"I know someone else just like that." Cadde knocked Kid's boots off his desk and they landed on the floor with a thud. "So what are you going to do?" he asked Chance.

"Nothing. I know Judd will call when the test results come in and he'll probably settle with Shay. As for me, my part is over."

"It's hell when the past comes back to haunt you," Kid remarked.

Cadde pointed a finger at him. "Remember that."

Kid grinned. "You know, Cadde, I was just in here and you weren't around. I thought hell had frozen over, because you're always here. And my past is my business."

"What did you want?" Cadde asked in an even tone.

"The Helms Number One has come in at a hundred barrels a day. That's great. Wouldn't Dad be proud?"

Chance had sent the numbers, so he knew the well was producing. But something about the awe in his brother's voice when he said "Dad" got to him, and the words bubbled to the surface before he could stop them. "How well did you know Dad?"

"What?" Kid looked puzzled. "I knew him as well as you or Cadde did."

"I didn't know him at all," Chance murmured.

"You're talking crazy," Cadde exclaimed. "What the hell is wrong with you?"

Suddenly Chance couldn't do it. He couldn't hurt them. "Nothing," he replied. "Forget I said anything." He headed for the door.

Kid kicked it shut before Chance reached it. "Oh, no. You started this and we're going to finish it."

"Sit down," Cadde said. "What's bothering you about Dad?"

Chance plopped into a leather chair and took a long, deep breath. "I've kept a secret for a lot of years and I've debated over and over whether to tell you. Considering how we felt about Dad, I thought it best not to."

"Why?" Cadde asked.

"It would hurt you too much."

Kid slapped Chance's shoulder. "Come on. We're grown men and we can take anything."

Maybe they could. Maybe he had blown the whole thing out of proportion. "I wasn't asleep the whole time in the backseat like I told the highway patrol. Mom and Dad yelling at each other woke me up."

"What were they yelling about?" Kid asked.

Chance looked down at his closed hands, feeling a pain as deep as he'd felt that night. "Dad told Mom he was leaving her for another woman. Said he had fallen in love. That he didn't mean for it happen, it just did." Chance drew a scorching breath. "Mom asked if he was leaving her and us boys. He said yes. That we were old enough to take care of ourselves. That's when Mom hit him, screaming over and over, 'Who is she?' He lost control of the car and it veered into the ditch and hit the tree. Flames shot out from under the hood and Mom screamed, 'Chance!' It was the last thing she said."

He paused for a second and suddenly couldn't breathe. It took a moment before he could say another word. "I jumped out and tried to open Mom's door but it was burning hot and wouldn't budge." Chance opened his hands and saw the scars that he would carry for the rest of his life.

Chapter Six

Total silence fell upon the room.

Cadde finally stood. "Who was the woman?"

"I don't know. Mom tried to get Dad to say who she was, but he wouldn't."

"Why have you kept this to yourself all these years?"

"I couldn't hurt you like I was hurt. But I'm tired of keeping secrets."

"Come on, Chance," Kid said. "Dad was a married man and he had a woman on the side. So what? A lot of men do that. I think it's almost normal."

Before Chance knew what he was doing, he was out of his chair and swinging his fist at his brother's jaw. The blow sent Kid flying to the floor. _____

Chance pointed a finger at his brother's shocked face. "Don't you dare make excuses for him. Ever! You didn't hear Mom crying. You didn't hear her screaming. You didn't hear her beg him not to go, and you didn't see her face against the car window, covered in blood…"

"Chance, calm down." Cadde patted his shoulder. "I don't think Kid meant it that way."

Their brother lumbered to his feet, rubbing his jaw. "I can speak for myself."

"Think about it, Kid," Chance said. "He was not only leaving Mom, he was leaving us. He'd put earnest money down on a house in Houston for his new love. He was leaving High Cotton and not coming back. The man who taught us about love, fidelity and life was a liar and a cheater. You may be able to laugh it off, but I can't—and haven't been able to for over twenty years."

"I'm not laughing it off," Kid growled. "I just need a reason he'd do something like that. I… I… God, how could he leave us?" The weight of the truth seemed to paralyze him.

"I need a drink," Cadde said. "Let's go to

the apartment and have a toast to dear ol' dad." He stopped by the table bearing the photo of the four of them. "He knew he was leaving when Mom took this." Suddenly, Cadde picked up the photo and slammed it against the wall, shattering the glass into a million pieces.

They stared at the broken shards for a moment and then walked out.

In the apartment, Cadde opened the liquor cabinet. "What'll it be, boys? Jack Daniels or some of Roscoe's best Kentucky whiskey?"

"I like the best," Kid said, sinking onto the leather sofa.

"Me, too," Chance replied, joining him.

Cadde poured the liquor and brought them each a glass, placing the bottle on the glass coffee table.

Kid took a swallow and rubbed the left side of his face. "I think you broke my jaw."

"You big baby," Cadde said, sitting in a large, comfy armchair.

"Who knew Chance had a mean right." Kid poured more whiskey.

"I'm not that scrawny kid you used to beat up," Chance told him.

"Yeah. I believe it."

Cadde held up his glass. "To dear ol' dad. May he rest in some sort of peace."

They clinked glasses and downed the whiskey.

Cadde stretched his long legs out in front of him. "All these years I've busted my ass to please Dad, but I realize now I wasn't doing it for him. I was doing it for myself. This is *my* dream."

"Here's to dreams," Chance said for a toast.

The more they drank the more they talked.

"Remember when I was dating Stacey Tullous in high school?"

"Yeah," Chance and Kid chorused.

"When things were getting a little serious, Dad said, 'Boy, you'd better keep your pants zipped. You don't want an unexpected pregnancy.' Then he went on about love and fidelity and to make sure she was the right one. He didn't want his boys to be adulterers. Hell, I was only sixteen."

"He told me the same thing about Lucinda Littlefield." Kid leaned his head against the leather. "I guess he didn't practice what he preached. I was just fourteen. I wasn't serious about anything."

"You're still not," Cadde told him.

Kid held up his glass. "Here's to I-don't-give-a-rat's-ass."

Chance looked at him. "You do know the receptionist is easy?"

"Hell, yeah." Kid took another swallow. "But a sure thing is better than sleeping alone after a long day." He looked down into his glass. "I wonder whatever happened to Lucky Littlefield. She hated it when I called her Lucinda."

Chance poured another round. "She's still in High Cotton. She left after high school, but came back when her dad fell ill."

"What does she look like now?" Kid asked curiously.

"Why?"

He shrugged. "Don't know. I was just thinking about her."

"She's not the same teenager who used to fawn all over you."

Kid raised his glass. "Now that's a pity."

Cadde poured more liquor. "Reality sucks."

"That's why I never told you." Chance knew what Cadde was talking about.

"Maybe it's a good thing you didn't. At sixteen, there's no telling what I would have done, but instead I pushed and pushed myself to succeed. Thanks to Roscoe I now own a big part of this oil company."

The room began to sway, and Chance had to squint to see Cadde. Wh-oh, he'd had too much booze. He heard a snore and saw that Kid was asleep with the glass in his hand. Chance put the glass on the table and the world faded away....

He awoke to the smell of coffee. Chance lay half on and half off the sofa, with his head against Kid's thigh. His brother was still out. Chance sat up and winced.

Cadde brought coffee to them. "Wake up, boys. It's a workday."

"Every day is a workday to you." Kid sat up, holding his head.

"What a pair of weaklings," Cadde teased, handing them each a cup of coffee.

"How come you don't have a hangover?" Chance asked.

"When you're in the oil business, you'd better learn to hold your liquor when you drink with the big boys."

"Who knew you were so talented," Kid muttered.

Chance took a sip of coffee, holding the cup with both hands. "My head is pounding."

"I can't feel mine." Kid tried to stand and fell back on the sofa.

Cadde sat in his chair nursing his coffee. "I don't know if we settled anything last night, but I think it's time to let Mom and Dad rest in peace."

"I feel a lot better getting it off my chest." Chance gingerly got to his feet.

"We'll never know what happened between them or what happened to Dad to make him change. It was personal and it was their lives. Now we have to let it go and live our lives our way, without bitterness or sadness."

"Who does he sound like?" Kid asked Chance.

"Dad," he answered, and laughed.

The three brothers hugged tightly for a long time. "We're gonna make it," Chance said at last.

And they would, he felt sure. The hole in his heart had shrunk considerably. He had done the right thing in telling them. Facing it together was much better than facing it alone.

Cadde was the first to pull away. "Now let's make Shilah the best independent oil company in Texas."

"You got it, big brother." Kid winced. "Just as soon as I can walk."

Chance laughed, and it felt good to laugh with his brothers. The past had truly been put to rest.

The beauty shop was full. Shay barely had time to run next door and fix her mother's lunch. Then Blanche wanted her back rubbed. After Blanche ate, Shay helped her to the bathroom. Making sure Blanche had her cell, she hurried back to the shop, ten minutes late for her next appointment.

It was Mrs. Beasley, who liked to express her opinions. But Nettie was entertaining her by reading her palm while her own customer was under the dryer. When Shay was a little girl Nettie had told her that she was half witch and half gypsy, and that she had magical powers. Darcy was now hearing the same stories.

Looking at Nettie, Shay believed she might be part gypsy or witch. Who knew? Nettie had a lot of fun with it. She wore long, full skirts and gypsy blouses, with lots and lots of jewelry. A colorful scarf was tied around her head and her gray hair, streaked with purple and green, flowed down her back. She was definitely different, and once people met her they never forgot her.

"I'm sorry I'm late, Mrs. Beasley," Shay said.

"That's okay." The seventy-years-plus woman got up and sat in Shay's chair. "Nettie was reading my palm. She said I was going to meet a stranger who would change my life. God, I hope it's a man. The one I've got is getting a little tiring."

Nettie winked at Shay.

Shay looked at Mrs. Beasley in the mirror. "We're coloring your hair today, right?"

"Yes." Mrs. Beasley ran her hands through the short gray strands. "I'm thinking I'd like to be a blonde."

"What?"

"Kind of like yours."

Had the woman lost her mind?

"Come on, Helen." Nettie joined the conversation. "You don't want to be a blonde. You'll have all these men chasing you and your husband will get jealous and leave. Then you'll have to go back to work to make a living."

"One of the other men will support me."

"Oh, no, honey," Nettie told her. "All they want is sex."

Mrs. Beasley's face turned a light shade of pink and she shifted uncomfortably in the chair. "What do you think, Shay?"

"I think your hair is lovely the way it is."

"Okay," Mrs. Beasley replied. "I'll keep it gray. I just wanted a change."

Don't we all.

"How about if we make it a lighter shade?" Shay asked.

"Oh, that sounds nice."

An hour later Mrs. Beasley gazed in the mirror at her new color. Shay held her breath.

"I love it!" the old lady exclaimed. "You always know what's best for me."

"Thank you," Shay replied. "It looks very nice."

"Herman likes it, too," Nettie added.

"Nettie, your husband has been dead for fifteen years. He can't see me and you can't hear him."

"Whatever."

They had the "Herman" conversation every week in the shop. Shay stayed out of it. If Nettie wanted to believe her deceased husband talked to her, that was fine with her.

Mrs. Beasley opened her purse, pulled out a wad of bills and placed them in Shay's hand. "I'll see you next week."

When she'd left, Shay straightened the money and counted it. "She gave me a ten-dollar tip, Nettie."

"She must really love that color." Nettie laughed.

Mrs. Kellis was in Nettie's chair now, getting curling rods put in for another tight perm. "Helen must be losing her mind," she commented. "A blonde? She should do something about all those wrinkles on her face."

Nettie held up her fingers like claws and hissed like a cat.

"I'm not being catty," Mrs. Kellis insisted. "But if you want to hear catty... Did you hear that Peggy down the street is cheating on her husband?"

Another cheating story. Shay sighed. Did anyone stay faithful?

The mailman walked in and Shay was glad. She didn't have to listen.

"Good afternoon, Shay," Ralph said. "I have a certified letter that requires your signature."

She scribbled her name on his electronic tablet and he handed her an envelope. Her eye went to the return address. The DNA test results. Now the Calhouns would know what she'd known since she was a child. Chance would, too. She had decided to put Chance out of her mind and out of her life. But why couldn't she stop thinking about him?

As she started to open it, Ralph said, "Here's the rest of your mail."

She took it and waved goodbye. Looking through the small bundle, she let out a scream. Quickly ripping open another envelope, she pulled out a check and waved it at Nettie. "My insurance company finally came through. Now I can buy a car."

"Good for you, hon," Nettie replied. "What's the certified letter about?"

"Just business stuff," she said, staring at Nettie and hoping she got the message. Shay didn't want to talk about the Calhouns in front of Mrs. Kellis. It would be all over the neighborhood in thirty minutes.

Glancing at her watch, she realized it was almost time for Darcy to come home from school. Shay busily started to clean the shop for the day. The putrid scent of permanent solution burned her nose, so she opened the small window to let in some fresh air.

She didn't know what she would have done if she hadn't had Nettie in her life. With her help, Shay had gotten her beautician's license and started working her way through college. She was starting her third year when her mother had become ill. There was no one else to take care of her; Blanche's lovers were nowhere in sight. When Blanche was down, she'd turned to her daughter for help. Shay couldn't say no, so she'd dropped out of school and worked at Nettie's to be close to home.

Nettie had converted her one-car garage into a beauty shop many years ago, and it was crowded and cluttered. A desk with a cash register stood at the front door. Shelves of beauty supplies covered a side wall. On the other wall were two hairdresser chairs and mirrors. Two hair dryers stood against the back, while to the right was a washer and dryer and sink for shampooing hair. Nettie had a colorful partition set up, but they could never wash towels while customers were in the shop. It was too noisy.

After gathering the dirty towels, Shay put them in the machine, for Nettie to turn on later. As she cleaned her station and swept the worn linoleum floor, her thoughts kept drifting. Her friend Beth had died about a year after Blanche had gotten sick. Shay had worked with Beth in an upscale beauty salon in Houston. Her friend had been in love with a loser, but Shay never told her that. When he heard about the baby, he'd told Beth she was on her own.

Beth had been devastated and Shay had helped her all she could. She was the first person to hold Darcy and was always there for babysitting. It had been rough, though, with Beth and Blanche sick at the same time. Shay didn't think life could get any worse, and then her friend had died. Shay was almost paralyzed with sadness.

It was a big adjustment for all of them, especially Blanche, who wanted all of her daughter's attention.

As Shay put the broom in the small closet, she saw the school bus drive up, and her heart beat a little faster. She loved Darcy as if she were her own.

She watched out the window as her adopted daughter jumped off the bus—alone. No Petey today. Darcy stomped toward the beauty shop, dragging her backpack behind her. Her face was scrunched into a frown. Something was wrong. Had she been disciplined again for talking too loud on the bus? No. It had to be something else.

Darcy walked in, dropped her backpack on the floor and sat in one of the dryer chairs with a pout on her face. The bruise on her lip had healed nicely.

"No hug?" Shay asked.

Darcy crossed her arms across her chest. "I don't feel like hugging."

Shay knelt in front of her. "What's wrong, sweetie?"

"Petey can't come to our house anymore," she muttered, trying very hard not to cry.

"Why not?"

"His mom says we spend too much time together and—and…" she slapped away a tear "…I get him into trouble all the time."

Shay saw red. How dare that woman hurt her child like this! She gathered Darcy into her arms, rubbing her back as Darcy sobbed against her shoulder. "Don't worry, sweetie, Mommy will take care of it."

Nettie put Mrs. Kellis under the dryer and looked down at Shay and Darcy sitting on the floor. "What's this I hear about Sally Henson?"

"She won't let Petey play with me anymore," Darcy cried.

Nettie placed her hands on her hips, her bracelets jangling. "Well, that's just mean. I think I'll turn her into a toad."

Darcy jumped up, all excited, her tears forgotten. "Can you, Nettie? Can you?"

Shay pushed herself to her feet. "No, she can't."

"You never know." Nettie winked.

Shay glared at the older woman. "Let's go home, sweetie, before I have to give Nettie a lecture."

"But it would be so cool, Mom," Darcy exclaimed, picking up her backpack.

Shay gathered her mail and then opened the door. Darcy ran toward their house, while Shay paused and looked back at Nettie. "If you really can, I'd appreciate it." She heard Nettie's laughter all the way home.

She got Darcy started on her homework and then checked on her mom. Blanche was sitting up in bed, watching TV.

"It's about time you came home," she shrieked through a round of coughs. "I want a cold glass of water with ice. Maybe you can get that right."

Another chipper day, Shay thought, and backed out. She walked across the hall to her room and closed the door. Pulling out her cell phone, she called Petey's mother.

"I knew you'd call," Sally said.

"When you hurt my kid, you better believe I'm calling."

"Before you get all angry—"

"I'm already angry."

There was a pause, and then Sally said, "I

heard about the incident with the boys next door. I won't have my kid being beat up because of Darcy's smart mouth."

Shay took a long breath to keep her anger in check. "Fine. If that's the way you feel, I suppose I can't change your mind. Just remember all the times I kept Petey and never charged you a dime. About six months ago you were in love with what's his name and I kept Petey day and night. Darcy and Petey play well together. It's when other kids tease them that bad things happen. I thought you were a friend, but I guess you're not." She clicked off before Sally could say another word.

Staring down at her phone, she drew another long breath. She was lousy at being a mother. Feeling her way was the best she could do.

"Shay," her mother screeched.

She jumped up and went to get the water.

After dinner, she let Darcy watch TV for a while. She seemed fine, but Shay knew she was going to miss Petey. At least she'd see him in school and on the bus.

Pouring a glass of tea, she noticed the mail on the counter. She picked it up and sat at the table to go through it.

She'd forgotten about the certified letter and ripped it open. It was just a single page. She glossed over the first part and glanced to the bottom—the result. *The probability that the alleged parent, Jack Calhoun, is biologically related to the woman, Shay Dumont, is 0%.*

She was *not* Jack Calhoun's daughter.

Chapter Seven

Chance had had a long day and was ready to get out of his work boots, take a shower and prop up his feet for a while. As he walked down the hall to the apartment, his cell buzzed. After looking at the caller ID, he clicked on.

"Hey, Judd, how's everything at the ranch?"

"Fine. I'm still looking for a foreman, though."

"You're not calling to…"

"To ask you to come back?" Judd finished. "Hell, no, I wouldn't do that to you."

"Thanks," Chance replied, feeling a moment of relief. He wouldn't want to let his friend down, and would have been torn if he'd asked.

"I thought I'd let you know I got the DNA results."

"And?"

A long pause ensued. "She's not Jack's biological daughter."

Chance stopped dead. "Damn. I wasn't expecting that. Shay was so sure—sure enough to try to steal those rings."

"We had a deal and I'm sticking to my word. I won't press charges."

"She'll appreciate that."

"Uh-oh."

"What?"

"The boys just waddled in. Eli, put that down. Cait, the boys are in my study."

Chance smiled. Sometimes Judd slipped into his father's way of thinking—that a woman's job was to take care of the kids and the house. Cait had a way of setting him straight and it didn't take her long.

"So?" Chance heard her shout. "I'm in the kitchen. Now we know where everyone is."

"She can be a smart-ass sometimes," Judd said to Chance. "I better go or they'll destroy my study. I need to buy a book on discipline. Justin, no…"

Chance laughed as he clicked off, and it felt good. For so many years laughing was hard for him. Now he was free from a secret that he shouldn't have kept at all. But the past was the past and he was now living in the present.

Unlocking the apartment, he went inside and headed to the bedroom. He took off his boots and saw Shay's green eyes. How was she taking the news? he wondered. She was positive about Jack's paternity, so it had to have hit her hard. He wanted to see if she was okay, but how could he? Shay was not a part of his life. She'd made that very clear.

He tore off his shirt on the way to the shower. He hardly knew the woman and yet he couldn't get her out of his mind. After he showered, he realized he was hungry. A steak sounded good so he drove to the Texas Roadhouse.

As he ate he looked around and saw that mostly couples occupied the tables and booths, clinking glasses, laughing and talking. A boisterous family sat in a corner. He was one of the few customers dining alone.

A man his age shouldn't be alone. There was always the receptionist, he thought, as he paid the check. Chance smiled as he went out the door. He would never be that desperate.

On his way back to Shilah Oil, it occurred to him that he was headed in the wrong direction. He was going north—to Shay. Damn truck had a mind of its own.

He parked in her driveway as dusk prepared to usher in the night. The neighborhood was quiet except for some loud music he could hear coming from down the street. He removed his hat and placed it on the passenger seat. After waiting a moment, he strolled to the front door and knocked.

Darcy opened it with the safety chain attached, reminding him of the first time he had come here. Tiny squeezed through the opened crack and sniffed at his boots.

"Is your mother home?" he asked.

"Yes."

"May I speak to her?"

"Depends," the girl answered.

"On what?"

"If I can sit in your truck."

He thrust a thumb over his shoulder. "That piece of junk?"

"Yeah," she replied without blinking.

"Hmm." Chance appeared to think about it. "Okay. We have a deal."

She quickly undid the chain and darted down the walk.

"Wait a minute," he called.

She stopped and looked at him. Her glasses were crooked. Did she ever keep those things straight?

"Don't sit on my Stetson and don't let that dog sit on it, either."

She frowned. "What's a Stetson?"

"My hat."

"Oh, okay." She ran to the truck and yanked on the door.

"And you can't stay out here long. It's getting dark."

Chance shook his head as he entered the house. Everything was quiet. The TV was on and Darcy's books were scattered in front of it. Where was Shay? He knew where the kitchen was so he went in that direction. Shay sat at the kitchen table, staring at a piece of paper.

"Shay."

She swung around and for a brief moment her eyes lit up when she saw him. The light was quickly replaced with a glare. "How did you get in here?" She was angry. That was very clear. He could tell by her heated words and stiff body.

"Darcy let me in."

"Where is she?"

"She's sitting in my truck. That's the deal we made so she'd let me in."

"You tricked her?" Shay's voice was hot enough to scorch his skin.

"No." He lifted an eyebrow. "I think she tricked me."

Shay gave him another red-hot glare. "I'll get her." She got up and tried to pass him. He stepped in front of her. She moved right and he stepped in front of her again.

Clenching her hands into fists, she said in a controlled voice, "Get out of my way."

"Not until you calm down."

"I'm calm," she told him, and wrapped her arms around her waist.

"Yeah, right." He touched the vein at her temple and she pulled away. "That vein is about to explode." He looked into her bright green eyes. "Why are you so angry? And don't say you're not."

She clamped her lips together and wouldn't say another word.

"You said the Calhouns meant nothing to you and you wanted nothing to do with them. So why has the truth made you so angry?"

"I've been lied to for so many years. I'm not the person I thought I was. I don't know who I am anymore." A tear slipped from her eye and his gut tightened. He hated to see her in so much pain.

He wrapped his hands around her upper arms and pushed her back into a chair. Pulling another chair forward, he sat facing her, their knees almost touching. "You're the same person I hoisted out of that creek. You're a beautiful, loving, compassionate woman who thinks of others instead of herself. You're Darcy's mother. Blanche's daughter. Everything is the same."

"No, it isn't. Everything's changed."

"Not everything."

Shay frowned. "What are you talking about?"

He linked his hands with hers and she didn't jerk away. "Every time you look at me with those green eyes all I want to do is kiss you."

She blinked. "You're...you're changing the subject."

He ran his thumb over her palm. "But you're calmer."

Her lips twitched into a smile. "You tricked me."

"Whatever works." He released her hand and pulled the paper from the lab forward.

"Talk to your mother…calmly, and get the truth for your own peace of mind."

Shay took a long breath, reached for the report and stood, her eyes on him. "Uh…for the record, you can kiss me anytime you want."

His heart flip-flopped and his breath hitched as he saw the truth in her eyes. Before he could move, the front door opened and closed, effectively ending the moment.

"Hey, look at me. I'm a cowboy." Darcy ran into the kitchen wearing his Stetson, Tiny yelping at her heels. No one wore his hat, and Chance wanted to remove it from her head, but he made no effort to do so. In that moment he knew he was in so deep with Shay that he was never going to find his way out—not that he wanted to.

"Where did you get that?" Shay asked Darcy.

"In his truck." She pointed to Chance. "It's a stepson."

"A Stetson," he corrected.

Shay smiled at Chance and then looked at her daughter. "Finish your homework. Mr. Hardin will help you with your spelling."

Chance did a double take. "What?"

"Does he know how to spell?" Darcy whispered.

Shay leaned down to her level. "I bet he does. I have to talk to Blanche, so be nice."

Chance and Darcy stared at each other and then she ran to get her homework.

"I have to write a paragraph…."

Darcy's words went right over his head. He wondered what was happening down the hall.

Shay opened her mother's door and closed it behind her.

"Oh, Shay. I was going to call you. Where's my nighttime medication?"

"In the nightstand drawer."

"Get it." Blanche's breathing wasn't so raspy tonight, so it was a good time to confront her.

"It's early for your medication."

"I'm tired and I want it now."

Shay walked closer to the bed. "First I want to talk."

Blanche frowned at her. "About what? I told you I'm tired."

"Explain this." She handed her the DNA results and her glasses from the nightstand.

"What is it?" Blanche whined.

"Read it and you tell me."

"Sometimes you can be a pain in the ass." Her mother slipped on her glasses and glanced at the paper. Her skin turned a sickly gray. "When did you take a DNA test and why?"

"I took it to prove to Judd that I was Jack Calhoun's biological daughter. I mean, I heard it every day of my life so I had no doubts. As your daughter I should be given your jewelry and half of Southern Cross. Wasn't that your plan?"

Blanche remained silent.

"I even tried to rob their house—perfect strangers! I could be in jail right now."

Still Blanche didn't speak.

"All you ever think about is Jack Calhoun. You dream about him at night. Tell me how you could cheat on a man you professed to love so much?"

Blanche threw the paper on the floor. Shay immediately picked it up and slapped it back on the bed. "Who is my father? My biological father?"

Blanche weakly waved a hand. "It doesn't matter. To me you were always Jack's child."

"It matters to me." Shay poked a finger into her chest, and then demanded, "Who is my real father?"

"I'm getting fed up with this, Shay. I'm ready to go to sleep."

"You're not closing one eye until I hear the truth—the whole truth."

Blanche didn't say a word, but Shay wasn't going to let her play possum. She was set on doing this now. "Mother..."

"Oh, okay." Blanche pushed herself up on the pillows. "I met him at one of those fancy parties Jack loved to attend to show me off. I was very beautiful in those days."

"I know," Shay murmured under her breath. She knew that better than anyone. Her mother had used her beauty to destroy.

"He was young, handsome, and I lost my head. Jack was being mean to me that night because I was dancing with the guy. He said I was acting like a whore out for a good lay, and if I didn't behave he was taking me home. He treated me like a child who needed to be told what to do. I was mad, and when the young man whispered in my ear to meet him upstairs, I did."

People in love didn't do things like that, did they? *Of course they did,* Shay told herself. How naive could she be? But that wasn't love... Shay wanted more—a forever love that didn't fade with time or suddenly disappear when someone younger and more exciting came along.

"It was a stupid decision that I regretted later, but I couldn't change what happened," Blanche said. "I thought Jack would never find out and life would go on as before. But evidently the maid saw us go into the bedroom, and told the wife of the man giving the party. The next time she saw Jack she told him. The bitch never liked me." Blanche coughed, trying to catch her breath.

Shay handed her a Kleenex to wipe her mouth.

"I came home one day from shopping and found a small suitcase at the back door. The door was locked and my key wouldn't work. Finally Jack unlocked it and told me to get off the ranch. He added that no one cheats on him. That was the last time I saw him. I begged and pleaded but he wouldn't listen." Blanche twisted the Kleenex in her hands.

"You never told him about me because you knew he'd have a DNA test done to prove paternity." Now some of the past was making sense.

"You're Jack's daughter. You are! You are! You are!" She pounded her fists on the bed and sank back against the pillows, completely out of breath.

Shay adjusted Blanche's oxygen and gave

her a few minutes. As she waited, she thought of how much of her mother's life was make-believe, and she had to wonder about Blanche's mental faculties.

"Who is my biological father?" Shay asked quietly.

Blanche pointed to some photo albums on a shelf. "Get…get me the brown leather one."

Shay did not want to look at photos of Jack and Blanche in their heyday, but she reached for the album and handed it to her mother. Besides bras, underwear and a few clothes, it was one of the items in the suitcase Jack had packed for Blanche. Evidently he hadn't wanted any photos of her left in the house.

Blanche flipped past pictures of her and Jack and finally pointed to one of a group of people. "That's your biological father."

Shay looked at the smiling young man. He was blond, his hair had a slight curl and he was tall compared to the other people in the photo.

"What color are his eyes?" Shay couldn't help but ask.

"Blue," Blanche replied. "A sparkling blue."

She bit her lip. "What's his name?"

"Eric Farnsworth." Her mother answered

without pausing. "That's his father standing to the left."

Shay looked at her grandfather. His hair was completely white and he had a regal bearing. But he didn't appear happy. Peering closer, she could see that Eric had his arm around Blanche's waist, and Jack was scowling. *The beginning of the end,* was all Shay could think. And the beginning of her life.

"Where does he live?" she asked in a faraway voice.

"He was from Dallas, but he died a year after I met him. He was an adventurer and loved mountain climbing. Money wasn't an issue with him. He lived off a trust fund from his grandfather."

Shay let out a hard breath. "How did he die?"

"He fell off a mountain in Nepal. I read it in the paper. He was estranged from his father because he wouldn't give up his wandering ways and settle down. The paper said that Mr. Farnsworth Sr. died of a massive heart attack when he heard the news."

"How sad," Shay murmured. Her real father had died when she was a baby. He'd known nothing about her.

As if Blanche could read her thoughts,

she added, "I should have told him about the baby. Then maybe some of the Farnsworth money would have come to me instead of going to charities. I didn't know how to get in touch with him, though. Besides, I wanted Jack back."

Shay's eyes narrowed on her mother's pale face. "You said you thought the baby was Jack's."

"It was." Blanche shook her head. "I mean, you are."

"Then why bother telling Eric?"

Her mother ripped the Kleenex to shreds. "Why did you have to take that test? Why did you have to break my heart?"

Blanche wasn't going to play the guilt card now. "You did that all by yourself without any help from me. Evidently Eric Farnsworth had money, and that attracted you. His looks only made the temptation that much stronger. You risked everything for one night with a stranger. I'm thinking things weren't going too smoothly for you and Jack and you wanted a backup man—someone with money. To you that's what love is—hard cash."

"When you grow up poor, money means everything." Blanche waved a hand around the drab room. "But I'm back where I started—living like poor white trash."

"We are not poor white trash," Shay snapped. "I work hard to keep a roof over our heads, food in our stomachs and clothes on our backs. I have money to buy what we need and sometimes to buy things we just want. I don't take charity or handouts—"

"Go do your rah-rah speech somewhere else," Blanche interrupted. "I'm tired."

Shay drew a long, silent breath. "Do you know how much you've hurt me?"

"Hurt you? How have I hurt you?"

"By repeatedly lying to me and depriving me of my biological father."

"Well, I never had a father either, so deal with it." Blanche turned on her side, away from Shay.

Shay tore the photo out of the album and left.

In her own room she sat on her bed and stared at the picture—stared at her father. He was a complete stranger, and no matter how many times she looked at his face, he was still a stranger. Unreal. Alien to her.

Was her mother lying? Blanche was good at that.

She glanced at her computer, and on impulse pulled out the desk chair. She typed in Eric Farnsworth and in an instant a charitable foundation popped up, with an address and a phone number.

Even though it was late she couldn't resist punching in the number on her cell.

She was startled when a voice answered, "Farnsworth Foundation."

"Ah… I'm looking for Eric Farnsworth." She didn't know what to say and the words came out in a rush.

There was a long pause. "I'm sorry, the Farnsworths are no longer living."

"Oh." Shay's hands shook, but she had questions and she wanted answers.

"Are there any living relatives?"

Another pause. "Mr. Farnsworth Sr. has a sister in a private nursing home, but dear, you can't apply for a charitable donation from a family member. Give me your charity's name and address and I'll mail you an application. But any request has to be approved by the board."

"Oh, no. That's fine. Thank you." Shay clicked off. Her courage stretched only so far. After her nerves calmed down, she realized one thing rang true. Her mother hadn't lied about Eric, and at least part of the story had checked out.

Shay buried her face in her hands. She'd made a fool of herself, believing her mother about the Calhouns. Never again would she go through that humiliation.

Who was she?

Shay Farnsworth. For a moment she let herself think about the name.

It was still alien to her. She wasn't Shay Farnsworth.

Shay Calhoun.

That certainly wasn't her.

Shay Dumont. That was her. She didn't need a father for a last name. She already had one. Taking one more look, she slipped the photo into a drawer.

Chance had said that nothing had changed, and it really hadn't. When she woke up tomorrow, she would still be Shay Dumont, with a small daughter to raise, a sick mother to care for and an eccentric cousin living next door. Yet she couldn't help but feel hurt and a little broken inside. She wouldn't be human if she didn't. But she wasn't going to wallow in self-pity. Her biological identity didn't change who she was.

Life would go on, of that she was certain.

But she was through dreaming about a father she would never meet. Blanche's lies had cured her of all those dreams.

And there was a tall, handsome cowboy waiting for her in the kitchen. His presence made this horrible day worth living through.

Chapter Eight

"What did you say?" Chance asked Darcy.

The girl let out an irritated sigh. "You're not listening. At least when Mom helps me, she listens."

"Okay, hotshot." He tipped back his Stetson, which she was still wearing, so he could see her face. "Tell me again. I'm listening."

She rolled her eyes. "I have to write a paragraph on the person I admire the most. Petey and me looked up the word *admire*. How's an eight-year-old supposed to know what that means?"

"But you had a good idea of what it meant, didn't you?"

"Yeah, but we wanted to be sure 'cause we make all A's and we didn't want to make a B."

Chance wondered where her sidekick was today, but figured the kid had to go home sometimes. He cleared his throat. "Have you written the paragraph?"

"Yes, and now you have to check my spelling." She slid a sheet of notebook paper toward him.

He glanced at her and asked, "Do you have a dictionary?"

She gave that annoyed sigh again. "I knew you didn't know how to spell."

"Get the dictionary," he said in a no-nonsense tone that had her out of her chair in an instant. While she was getting it, he read her paragraph.

"I admire my mom the most. She's not my reel mom but she's still my mom. She cooks for me, buys my cloths and makes sure I have everything I need. She works reel hard and never complanes. I admire my mom the most cause she's my mom and no one else's."

Chance smiled. He kind of admired her mom, too.

Darcy ran back and plopped a red *Webster's* on the table. As she sat down, he pushed the paper to her. "I circled the words that are misspelled."

"You wrote on my paper?" she asked in outrage.

"Yes. What's the problem?"

"I have to write it over."

"So? It's one paragraph. If it takes you more than five minutes, you're in trouble."

She glared at him.

"Oh, I see. You were going the old erase-and-change route, huh?"

"Yes," she mumbled.

"That's messy. You do not get an A by being messy."

She looked at him, her glasses lopsided. "Do you have kids?"

"No."

"Good," she said, in a tone that implied how lucky the world was.

"Check the words," he instructed in his stern voice again.

With a thoughtful look, she pushed her glasses up the bridge of her nose, and he knew something was percolating in that mischievous brain of hers. "Why don't you tell me how to spell them? It'll be faster."

He nudged the dictionary toward her. "Look them up." When she made no move to open it, he added, "Now!"

She grabbed the book and started searching. "I know I have that one right. Shucks, I don't."

After she corrected each one, he placed a clean sheet of paper in front of her. "Now write it over."

Without a word, she began to do so, chewing on her tongue all the while.

"Petey can't come here anymore," she said out of the blue, still working on her paragraph.

"Why not?"

"Because I get him in trouble all the time, his mom says." The little girl made an I-don't-like-her face. "Nettie's going to turn her into a toad. Yeah, that's gonna be cool—so cool."

Chance had no idea what she was talking about, but decided not to open that door. Some things were better left unsaid.

She stopped working on the paragraph and he tapped the paper. "You're not through."

"Okay, okay," she grumbled, and went back to work.

Suddenly she stopped again. Peering up at him, she said, "Shay's not my real mom."

Damn, the girl switched gears faster than that old Mustang he and Kid had fixed up. With a smooth stretch of highway and not a cop in sight they could go zero to ninety in…

He caught her impatient stare and applied the brakes on his wandering thoughts. He cleared his throat. "I know."

"My real mom died when I was four. I miss her, but I don't…" She paused and twisted her pencil between her fingers.

"You don't what?" Chance asked.

"I don't remember her much. Is that okay?"

He leaned forward, his heart in his throat. "Yes, it's okay. I was twelve when my mom died, and sometimes it's hard to remember certain things." But he vividly remembered her bloody face against the car window. He could also still hear her screams. Those things were etched in his mind—forever. But he wouldn't tell Darcy that. Her situation was different.

"Really?" she asked, her eyes bright behind the glasses.

"Yes, really. It's perfectly normal."

"Shay's my mom now."

He knew exactly where Darcy was going. "You can love Shay all you want. Your mom doesn't mind."

"Good." Darcy went back to her paragraph.

Tiny jumped up and barked at the back door. A woman walked in. Chance blinked and wondered if he was seeing correctly. She wore a long, flowing, colorful skirt with some sort of puffy blouse. A bright sash and beads adorned her waist and a scarf was tied around her long gray hair. Were those purple and green streaks for real…? Yes, they were. She had on more jewelry than he'd seen in his life, so much that she jangled when she walked.

"Hey, Nettie," Darcy said, without raising her head.

"Where's your mother?"

The girl gestured over her shoulder. "With Blanche."

The woman's gaze swung to him. "Oh, I didn't know you had company."

Chance stood and walked over to her, holding out his hand. "I'm Chance Hardin."

She shook hands with a wide-eyed stare. "Chance Hardin, you say."

"Yes."

"Does Shay know you're here?"

"Yes," Darcy answered. "He's helping me with my homework."

"Oh," she said, her gray eyes puzzled.

Before he could respond, Shay walked into

the living room. Chance watched her face. She looked okay, but was she?

Nettie hurried to her and he could hear them whispering, but he couldn't hear what they were saying. Suddenly they hugged, and Nettie jangled out the door.

Shay turned and stared at him then, and, abruptly, the hum of the refrigerator sounded like an eighteen wheeler rolling through the house. He saw so many things in her eyes: sadness, heartache and pain. Amid the pain was hope. She was going to make it. She was going to be fine.

She was the first to look away. "Have you finished your homework?" she asked Darcy.

"Yeah, but I had to write it over 'cause he—" Darcy pointed her pencil at him "—wrote on my paper."

"Why did Chance do that?"

"Well…" Darcy was flustered. Clearly, she hadn't expected her mother to ask that question.

"You were going to erase the mistakes and rewrite, weren't you?"

Darcy nodded.

"You know I don't allow that. It's messy and your teacher will take off marks for it."

"Yeah." Darcy gathered her papers. "Adults all think alike."

"Yes, we do," Shay told her. "Put your papers and books in your backpack so it will be ready for school in the morning, and then go take a bath. I'll tuck you in when you're through."

"Okay." Darcy darted off with Tiny at her heels, but not before Shay snatched Chance's hat from her head.

"I think this belongs to you." She handed it to him and sat at the table.

"Are you okay?" he asked, twisting the Stetson in his hands.

"I'm not sure. It all feels so unreal, as if I'm watching a movie or something, and I'm emotionally detached from it." She told him about her conversation with Blanche.

"Wow!" He sat beside her. "That's some story. You called the Farnsworth Foundation?"

She scrunched up her nose. "Pretty desperate, huh?"

"It's very human to be curious."

"Mmm. Mom has told me so many lies I had to be sure this time. But it's my life— how I was conceived, not in love but in lust." Saying the words out loud made it seem more real to her, but made her nerves ping-pong with restlessness. She stood. "Would you like something to drink? Coffee, tea or a soft drink?"

"A glass of iced tea would be nice," he replied.

She picked up her glass from the table and reached for another in the cabinet. After opening the refrigerator for the tea, she poured two glasses. Setting one in front of him, she sat down again.

He reached for her hand, and for a moment she tensed. But then she felt his strength, his power, and she wanted to lean on him, let him absorb some of the shock from years of lies.

"You're all wound up," he remarked, caressing her clenched fist until she opened her hand. As he placed his large palm against hers, a wave of new sensual feelings washed over her. "Take a deep breath, calm down and talk to me. Talking is a great healer. I found that out just recently." His voice was soothing. Comforting. Real.

Her whole body relaxed as he went on to tell her the story of his parents' deaths and the secret he'd kept.

"Oh, Chance." She gripped his hand with

both of hers, trying to ease his pain. "I'm sorry you had to go through that."

"You're trembling."

She'd hoped he wouldn't notice, but hearing about his parents and the other woman was just too much for this day.

"I'm a little emotional," she tried to explain.

"It's okay," he said, and she felt worse. "You're sort of the reason I finally told my brothers."

"Me?"

"Yes. I got a glimpse into how secrets can destroy people's lives, and I knew I had to tell my brothers the truth."

"Oh." Tears stung the back of Shay's eyes. Chance Hardin was the nicest, most handsome, most tempting man she'd ever met. She didn't deserve him.

"I'm sure your mother thought she was doing the right thing. After all, neither man was in your life, nor were they likely to be."

"That's true." His soothing voice pulled Shay in and she found herself confiding in him. "Blanche never thought about me. It was all about her and the money. That's what made her happy—money." More words came tumbling out. Words that peeled away layers of her life she always kept to herself. She found herself telling him about her lonely childhood, about Nettie raising her and about her mother's many lovers. Like an onion, each layer seemed to grow more potent, more revealing of who she was at the center of her heart.

"I guess I was about ten or eleven when I figured out the male and female relationship. When Mom would bring one of her lovers home, I'd sneak out the back door to Nettie's. I didn't want to be in the house when she had men over. It made me feel creepy."

In the silence that followed, he asked, "One of them didn't…"

"Abuse me?" Shay shook her head. "I was never around them that long, and if one had dared, Nettie would have put a curse on him so strong he'd never be able to function again."

Chance smiled and Shay's heart wobbled. That smile could open doors, melt ice and heal the deepest wounds. There was power and magic in his lips. She'd heard Nettie say that once about her late husband and Shay was seeing it now.

With that smile Chance could make her

believe in fairy tales, the Easter bunny and Santa Claus.

And just maybe, love.

"A curse?" He lifted an eyebrow.

She raised a shoulder in jest. "Nettie professes to be a gypsy witch, but that's a whole other story."

"She's…different."

"Yes," Shay replied, and actually laughed at his careful choice of words.

After all the layers had been peeled away, the potency that was left was real. A lonely, frightened little girl had turned into a strong woman. A survivor. *Shay Dumont.* Nothing would change that. Her life wasn't perfect— no one's was. But it was her life. She'd managed to survive a difficult childhood and she would survive now. That was the honest truth, deep in her heart. Learning about her real father hadn't changed a thing. She already knew who she was.

"Mom," Darcy called.

"I'll be back," Shay said, getting to her feet. "I have to put my daughter to bed."

After listening to Darcy's prayers, she kissed her good-night and hurried back to Chance. He stood in the kitchen, his hat in his hand.

When he saw her, he placed his Stetson on his head and said, "It's getting late. I better go."

"Oh." She didn't want him to leave. She wanted to explore all these feelings she had when she was with him, even though her heart told her it was dangerous. But after the revelations of today she'd come to see that each day was a gift and a risk. Blanche took risks without hesitation. But could Shay?

"May I ask you a question?" Chance murmured, interrupting her musings.

"Of course," she replied. His face was set in a neutral mask, but she knew he didn't feel that way. What did he want to know? She wondered nervously.

"Why didn't you call me the day you took the DNA test? I gave you my number."

So that was it. She decided to be honest, because at the moment that was all she could muster. "I thought about it and I wanted to, but I don't have time to get involved with anyone. My life's a mess and I have to concentrate on Darcy and her future. I can't just leave her to go on a date."

"So you deprive yourself of a life of your own?"

"For now, yes."

"That's not normal, Shay, and you know it. If you allowed yourself to have some fun, you'd be better equipped to handle the stress at home."

"After today I'm not sure about anything."

He looked straight at her and the darkness of his eyes made her insides quiver with need. "I meant what I said earlier about kissing you. I've been attracted to you since pulling you out of that creek. I know you feel the same way. When I first walked in here, your eyes lit up when you saw me. Let's build on that feeling. I'm not asking a lot—just a simple date."

The temptation, oh, how sweet it was. All she had to do was say yes, and her life would change. She'd be involved with the one man who could break her heart. And if he knew the truth, she most definitely would break his. She wasn't like her mother. She couldn't hurt other people for her own satisfaction.

"I can't," she whispered, the words burning her throat. She couldn't take the risk.

"Fine," he said in a clipped tone as he walked past her to the front door.

He was leaving, walking out of her life. That thought jarred like no other. The one thing that was good in her life was leaving, and she'd never see him again. But that was the way it should be—no one would get hurt.

Shay wrestled with her conscience. She wrestled with the truth and with her heart. In a few short seconds she understood how she was like her mother. The temptation was too great, the loss too severe. She never thought of herself as a gambler, but was willing to take the risk. It was better than being alone.

"Chance."

He turned at the door to stare at her. A rash of nervousness hit her, but she didn't change her mind. She walked closer to him, grabbing her courage in her hands. "Earlier you asked if I was okay." She swallowed. "I'm not. I need someone to hold me."

He stretched out his arms and she ran into them. Drawing her body against his, he smoothed his hand up her back to her hair, and weaved his fingers through her tresses. Her hair clip popped off, but neither noticed.

He kissed her neck and she trembled with pleasure, breathing in his masculine scent. "Why are you making this so hard?" he whispered.

It was impossible to think with his lips on her skin, but she tried. "I don't want Darcy growing up like I did feeling alone and scared because my mother was never there. I have to be here for Darcy so she knows I love her and that she always comes first."

"She already knows that," he murmured against her ear. "No matter what you do you're not going to get parenting exactly right. As far as I can tell no one has mastered it yet. You're just paranoid because she's not your biological child."

"I suppose…" Shay gasped as his lips traveled across her cheek to her mouth, then with fierce need they took hers. She stood on tiptoes and wrapped her arms around his neck, feeling his strength and his power as a man. It was so tempting, so potent that she had no problem giving in to her every impulse. Giving in to Chance. To the inevitable. The kiss deepened in intensity. Emotions, denied too long, came to life, locking them in their own private world.

He rested his forehead against hers. "When can I see you again?" he asked in a hoarse tone, and he seemed to be holding his breath as he waited for her answer.

"I have to buy a car tomorrow. Would you like to come with me?"

"You bet. And maybe we can have lunch."

"That would be nice."

He pulled her closer, if that was possible, and kissed her deeply, bracing his back against the wall. She was glad he was holding her or she would have crumpled into a mass of quivering pleasure at his feet. She leaned into him feeling every hard muscle of his lean body. Her senses experienced new delights, but she knew they had to stop. They were reaching a point of no return and they both were aware of it.

"I have to go," he breathed into her mouth.

"Yes."

He weaved his fingers through her hair again and held her head. Kissing her one more time, he said, "See you tomorrow."

"Yes."

"What time?"

"About ten. I have to turn in the rental, too."

Again he rested his forehead against hers. "I have to go," he repeated.

He didn't move. Not that she wanted him to. But he had to.

As with a child's toy, she gave him a slight push to get him started. She couldn't help but laugh. He echoed her laughter and strolled down the walk.

The moonlight cast long shadows across

the lawn, engulfing Chance. She watched until his taillights were out of sight. Then the darkness crowded in on her.

As a child she'd been afraid of the dark. It was something she couldn't define or explain, and seemed to devour everything around her. She had called it the "monster." Blanche was never too concerned about her phobias. When Nettie had voiced concern, Blanche had said that Shay would outgrow them. And she had. The monster had been slain with maturity.

She went inside and closed the door. She didn't agonize over what had happened with Chance. And she didn't agonize over what was going to happen tomorrow or the next day. No one knew what life was going to bring. She was betting on happy ever after. Some would say that was like betting on a horse with a broken leg.

But now she was willing to take the risk.

Chapter Nine

Shay woke up early the next morning, as excited as a teenager going on a first date. Last night had been wonderful. Today would be better. Beyond that she wouldn't think.

Since it was Saturday, she let Darcy sleep in and went to get the paper. Out on the sidewalk she stopped short. A large frog sat in the grass. She peered closer. Was that a toad? Nah, she told herself, and picked up the paper.

Not able to resist, she stopped by the frog again. She looked left and right to make sure no one was watching her, then leaned down and asked, "Sal, is that you?"

The frog croaked deep in its throat and

hopped toward Nettie's house. "You're going in the right direction. Be nice and she might turn you back." Shay laughed all the way into the house. It was fun to be silly.

She hurriedly fixed Blanche's oatmeal and placed it on a tray with coffee, orange juice and a banana. As she opened Blanche's door, she saw her sitting on the side of the bed.

"I heard someone laughing," Blanche said.

"That was me being silly." She placed the food on a TV tray. "Breakfast time."

"I have to go to the bathroom first."

"Okay. Do you feel like walking?"

"Yes." Blanche removed the oxygen from her nose and tried to stand. Shay came to her aid and helped her into the bathroom. Blanche was breathing heavily by the time they walked back, and Shay quickly started the oxygen again.

She placed the tray in front of her mother. "Try to eat as much as you can." Blanche ate very little these days.

Blanche stirred the oatmeal with a thoughtful look. "Despite our talk last night, you're very chipper this morning."

"Being angry and bitter will accomplish nothing. I can't change the past."

"You're Jack's child to me and I'll never forgive you for taking that DNA test."

"That's a cross I'll have to bear," Shay said in a dramatic tone of voice.

"You're different. You're not getting angry." Blanche's eyes narrowed. "I heard a man's voice last night. Who was here?"

"Chance Hardin," Shay replied without hesitation.

"What did he want?"

"Nothing. He just came to see me."

"Why?"

Shay placed her hands on her hips. "Well, I like him and he likes me. 'Nough said."

Blanche took a swallow of coffee. "You're getting in over your head and you know it. Break it off."

Shay straightened the bed, ignoring her mother's words. "I'm going to look for a car this morning. Nettie will be here."

"That old bat. I'm surprised she hasn't sprouted wings by now."

"Nettie has been very good to us...."

"Yada, yada, yada." Blanche waved off her little lecture.

Shay took a deep breath. "Is there anything else you need?"

"Yes," Blanche retorted. "My rings."

Not again. Not ever again.

"It should be easy for Mr. Hardin. Judd respects him and will honor his request."

"They're material things," Shay told her. "Why do they mean so much to you?"

"They are a symbol of Jack's love."

"Oh, please. From what I've learned of the man, he loved no one but himself."

"Jack was difficult sometimes, but always generous."

The money again.

"Yes, well, we're all grateful for that," she said in a sarcastic tone, and not willing to sink that low, she added, "I have to fix Darcy's breakfast and get dressed. I'll be home as soon as I can."

Blanche pointed a spoon at her. "You tell Nettie I don't want to hear any gypsy crap, and you might remind her that you're my daughter—not hers."

"Pity you didn't remember that when I was about five, eight, twelve, fifteen…."

"Go away!" Blanche shouted as loudly as she could manage, then broke into a coughing fit.

"Gladly."

On the way to the kitchen it hit Shay that her mother cared about her, but had never learned how to show it—to accept it. Blanche knew only one kind of love—sexual. She had mastered that, but any type of loving relationship with her daughter or Nettie seemed impossible. Ironically, though, when she needed help Blanche always turned to Shay and Nettie.

Shay put her mother out of her mind and mixed blueberry pancakes for Darcy. It was Saturday's breakfast—their special time.

"I smell pancakes," Darcy cried, running into the kitchen in her Barbie pajamas, with Tiny yelping at her feet. In her arms she held an old teddy bear she'd had since she was a baby—a connection to her mother.

Darcy knelt in a chair while Shay placed the food on the table.

"This is our special time, isn't it, Mommy?"

"Yes, sweetie," Shay replied, cutting Darcy's pancakes and slathering them with syrup. "But remember Mommy has to look for a car today?"

"Yeah. I'm gonna stay with Nettie and she's gonna paint my fingernails and toenails. Can I choose any color?"

"Yes, you may," Shay answered, downing a mouthful of pancake. "Just don't let her do anything crazy."

Darcy munched on a slice of bacon. "Like what?"

"Like dyeing your hair orange."

"No way." The girl giggled and syrup ran down her chin. Shay quickly wiped her mouth, as if Darcy were two years old. Sometimes it was hard to curb those motherly impulses. But today Darcy didn't remind her that she wasn't a baby.

Shay glanced at the clock. "I have to get dressed or I'm going to be late."

"Get us a red car without a top," Darcy suggested.

"I'm not buying a convertible," she said, carrying dishes to the sink.

"Get one with a Hemi then."

"Cars don't have Hemis."

"Shoot."

Nettie's arrival prevented more suggestions, and Shay was relieved.

"I'm sorry about the dishes, Nettie, but I have to run. Everyone has had breakfast."

"Don't worry, Herman and I will do them."

Darcy looked up at Nettie. "Herman's dead. He can't wash dishes."

Sad to say, they had this conversation quite often. Nettie swore on a stack of bibles that she could see her Herman. He was with her at all times.

Darcy held out her arms, grasping at thin air. "Where is he, Nettie? Where?"

"Oh, child, I'm the only one who can see him."

Darcy snapped her fingers. "Shoot."

Shay shook her head on the way to her bedroom. This wasn't normal, but it was as normal as her life would ever get. And Herman didn't hurt a soul.

Yanking open her closet door, she began to pull out clothes. What was she going to wear? Her hand paused over a pair of sleek black slacks she'd bought at Chico's and had never worn. Her life called for jeans and T-shirts, and the slacks were a little dressy, but she planned to wear them today. But first she had to put up her hair in hot rollers. After that she slipped on the pants and grabbed a white knit top with three-quarter-length sleeves and a buttoned front.

She was unsure about what shoes to wear and decided on black heels. As she shoved her feet into them, she started taking out the rollers. In less than five minutes she was ready to go.

But first she had to call Chance. She'd

memorized the number just in case she lost it. That might have been a dead giveaway about her feelings for him.

"Good morning," he said, and she sank onto the bed, letting that deep, velvety drawl roll over her. He sounded *so* good.

"Could you pick me up at the rental place?" She rattled off the address.

"No problem. Just so you're not canceling."

"I'm not canceling."

"See you in a few minutes."

Chance clicked off with a smile. He'd almost been afraid to answer—afraid she would cancel. But not today. He reached for his keys as Cadde stomped in. He had a growth of beard, his tie was askew and his hair was standing on end.

"What the hell happened to you?"

Cadde blinked. "Nothing. Why?"

"You look like hell."

"I've been working."

"All night?" Chance asked.

"What time is it?" His brother squinted at his watch.

"It's after nine in the morning, you idiot."

"So? I work late a lot."

"This isn't late," Chance informed him.

"This is insane. What was so important that it couldn't wait until tomorrow?"

"I was going over all of Roscoe's old leases, leases that Shilah holds the rights to, and to my surprise I found several in the Eagle Ford area. With the new drilling technology we could reenter those plugged wells. Eagle Ford is hot now and if we drill below the Austin Chalk, our dividends could be huge. I just have to get it past the board."

"Then why aren't you home talking about this with Jessie? She's the board member with the power."

Cadde ignored the question and sank onto the sofa, rubbing his stubbled chin. "I need a shave, a shower and some sleep."

"But not here," Chance said in a firm tone. "This is my home for now, and I'd appreciate it if you'd respect my privacy and not storm in here anytime you please. I might have had someone here."

"Oh." Cadde ran a hand through his already tousled hair. "The lady with the green eyes? Shay something?"

"Maybe." The odds of getting Shay to the apartment were slim to rock-bottom nothing. But that didn't matter. He just enjoyed being with her, and he understood her worries concerning Darcy. He'd never ask her to do anything that would make her uncomfortable.

Cadde stood. "I'll shower and sleep on the sofa in my office."

Chance wanted to laugh at the picture that created in his mind. Cadde was bigger than the small antique sofa, and sleeping on it would be a joke.

"Never mind," Chance said. "I'm going out, anyway. But please call before you burst in here again."

Cadde saluted in a smart-ass way and took a step toward the hall as Kid walked in.

"Hey, Chance, have you seen—"

"Have you ever heard of knocking?" He stopped his brother midsentence.

"What?" Kid looked baffled.

"When you enter someone's home, you knock," Chance told him. "It's polite. Remember all those manners Mom taught us?"

Kid peered closely at him. "Are you drunk?"

"No. But I could use a stiff drink when dealing with you two."

Kid shook his head as if to shake Chance from his mind. "I was looking for Cadde."

Chance waved a hand toward his older brother. "Well, you've found him."

"No, he hasn't," Cadde growled. "I'm going to sleep."

"Mr. Swenson has agreed to lease his land—to Shilah Oil."

"What?" Cadde swung around. Kid had his full attention. "The Swenson tract that every oil company in Texas has been trying to lease? He agreed to lease to an independent?"

"Yep." Kid rocked back on his heels, very pleased with himself.

"Damn, Kid, that's…" Cadde stopped. "Wait a minute. You didn't sleep with his daughter, did you? You two were making a lot of eye contact the last time we visited Mr. Swenson."

"Nah. I took her out to dinner, though."

Cadde groaned and Chance knew a whole lot of yelling was about to ensue—yelling about business ethics, morals and what-the-hell-were-you-thinking. He could see it building in Cadde's puffed out chest.

Kid felt it, too. He edged toward the door. "Now, Cadde, we didn't talk about the lease. It was never mentioned." At the thunderous look in Cadde's eyes, he added, "We'll talk about this when you're more reasonable." And like a puff of smoke he was gone.

"I need a damn drink," Cadde said, and headed for the liquor cabinet.

Chance thought this was a good time to leave, too. Listening to Cadde yell on a Saturday morning was unholy, somehow. As he closed the door he heard Cadde shout, "Look for a place to live today. I want this apartment back."

Not today, big brother. I have plans with a green-eyed lady.

Chance drove up to the car rental place on West Holcombe. Shay's rental was parked to the side, but he didn't see her. A blonde was talking to a man. Other than that no one else was around.

The blonde shook hands with the guy and strolled Chance's way. He looked closer. The gorgeous blonde was Shay. He'd never seen her all decked out. Wow! He could only stare. Blonde curls cascaded around her face like a movie star's. In black slacks and heels, her body was free-flowing, almost liquid.

She opened the door and slid into the passenger's seat. The cab of the truck filled with the scent of lavender and the scent of her. His loins tightened.

Buckling her seat belt, she glanced at him. "You're staring. Did I smear my lipstick?"

"Not that I can tell, but I'd like to smear it."

She laughed and reached out to touch his face. Her hand lingered and the pilot light to his senses burst to life.

"I've never seen you all dressed up," he managed to say.

She tossed her curled tresses. "I thought I'd bring my own arsenal to combat sleazy salesman tactics."

"They don't stand a chance," he said, and backed out.

They went to several dealerships, but she couldn't find what she was looking for. Everything was too expensive. She liked a silver Tahoe that was fully equipped, but said it was way out of her price range. Her eyes kept straying to it as she looked at other cars. If she would let him, he'd buy it for her, even though he was short on cash. But that wasn't a possibility. He knew her well enough to know she would never accept it.

She settled on a white Chevy Impala that seemed perfect for her. And the price was right. The salesman said they would wash and clean the car and it would be ready after lunch.

As they climbed into the truck, he asked, "Where would you like to go for lunch?"

"I don't know. Anywhere is fine," she replied.

"Anywhere?"

She laughed, a tingly sound that warmed his senses and other places. "I don't go out that much, so if it's not McDonald's, I'm lost."

"We're not going to McDonald's."

"Thank you." She leaned over and kissed his cheek. He loved it when she did spontaneous things like that, but it was hell on his driving, not to mention his concentration. "Oh, look, there's a carnival." She glanced back at the amusement rides. "I can't remember the last time I was on a Ferris wheel."

He turned off TX 288 and drove under an overpass.

"Where are we going?" she asked.

"To a carnival."

"You're kidding." Even though she appeared to object, there was a gleam of excitement in her eyes.

"Nope." It was Saturday, so the area close to a strip shopping center was packed with parents taking their children. The parking lot was also full, but he found a spot.

Removing his hat, he asked, "Ready?"

"Ready," she echoed with a smile.

Hand in hand they walked toward all the excitement. He bought tickets and they mingled with the kids and teenagers. A fortune teller tried to lure them over, but they kept walking, listening to some offbeat music and the squeals and laughter from the rides.

When they reached the Ferris wheel, Chance handed the man their tickets and they stepped in line for the next seat. The huge wheel turned and a double seat came down to their level. The man opened the bar and they climbed inside, sitting side by side. Chance looped his arm across her shoulders, pulling her to his side. She snuggled against him, and nothing had ever felt so right in his whole life.

The wheel stopped again for four teenagers, and then they were off for the ride of their lives. As the wheel went higher and faster, Shay squealed and burrowed into him. He laughed and held on tight.

"Oh, that was wonderful," Shay said as they climbed out.

"You never lifted your head."

"So? It's much more fun to clutch a handsome cowboy." She ran her hands through her tousled hair and for a moment he couldn't looked away.

He bowed from the waist. "I stand corrected, and the cowboy enjoyed the clutching."

She laughed and he slipped his arm around her waist as they tried to make their way to the exit. Kids were running, yelling and generally having a good time.

Suddenly Shay stopped. "Hot dogs. I love carnival hot dogs."

"No, no." He shook his head. "I want to take you to a nice restaurant."

"But I love hot dogs!" She slipped her fingers between two buttons on his shirt and touched his skin. "Please."

At her touch he was sure the whole place had gone up like a fireworks display on the Fourth of July. It was that riveting. In that moment he knew he'd do anything she asked—even eat a hot dog.

"What kind?" he asked, watching the light dance in her green eyes.

"Chili cheese, of course."

"Of course." He walked to the stand and she squeezed into a spot at one of the tables that had been strewn about.

As he waited for the hot dogs he thought about his father. Had his new love been that irresistible, that tempting—like Shay? Had he completely lost his mind over her that he was willing to give up his sons and his sons' mother? Yes, Chance could see it now. A woman had an uncanny way of bending a man to her will. He felt it with Shay—the pull, the attraction. All he could think about was being with her. He'd probably do anything she asked, but he did have some common sense.

His father had been older, and maybe just tired of resisting someone he really wanted. It was the first time Chance had made an excuse for his dad.

And it would be the last.

Chapter Ten

Chance munched on his hot dog and watched Shay devour hers. She really loved hot dogs.

Wiping her mouth, she asked, "Do I have chili on my face?"

"Yes," he said, and leaned over and licked it off, managing a slow kiss at the same time.

A bubble of laughter left her throat. "People are watching us."

"I'm not licking their chili off," he said with a straight face.

She laughed out loud and covered her mouth. Resting her elbows on the table, she cupped her face in her hands. "Do you know how wonderful you are?"

"No. But you can tell me." The light in her eyes was about to blind him.

"Being with you makes me happy. Usually I go through a routine each day, and happiness is not part of it. I love Darcy, and caring for her is a little bit of heaven, but pleasure for myself is very rare. Today has been special because of you."

"I must make a note to feed you hot dogs every day."

She laughed again and stood. "And you make me laugh."

He threw their trash into the garbage container and slipped his arm around her waist again. Slowly, they walked toward the entrance. On the way, he bought her cotton candy, and they laughed like teenagers as they ate the sugary treat.

It was that kind of day—fun and special.

Once inside the truck she fished her phone out of her purse and called Darcy and Nettie to check how things were at home. She told them she was waiting for her car and she'd be home soon. Then she called the dealership to see if her car was ready. It wasn't.

"Another hour or so," she told him. Watching her, Chance knew Shay wasn't the type of woman his father had gotten involved with.

Shay was too loving, too caring. She could never hurt anyone. Her care of Darcy and Blanche proved that.

As he had so many times in the past twenty-two years, he wondered about the woman who had tempted his father away from his family. Where had he met her? Chance quickly pushed the thoughts from his mind.

He ran his hand over the steering wheel. "Since we have time, would you like to see Shilah Oil? This is not a do-you-want-to-see-my-etchings type question."

"I'd love to see Shilah Oil, and it never crossed my mind."

It had crossed his about a hundred times.

From US 59 he turned onto San Jacinto, headed for Louisiana Street. It took less than fifteen minutes.

Shay looked up at the tall building. "I'm impressed. Where's your office?"

He pointed to the top floor. "For now I live up there, too."

"You live in your office?"

"No." He smiled when she frowned. "Roscoe Murdock, the founder of the company, had his own private apartment installed for when he worked long days and was too tired to go home. Cadde's letting me stay there until I can find a place."

"This Roscoe doesn't mind?"

"No. He died a few months ago."

"Oh."

"I'd take you up, but you know what's going to happen if I do."

She looked at him, her green eyes dark. "You'll show me your etchings? Then we'll kiss and get lost in what we're feeling."

Her honesty blew his mind. "I don't think you're ready for that."

One eyebrow lifted. "Try me," she said and then burst out laughing. "Darcy has this stuffed dog that has a little round button on it that says Try Me. You push the button and he barks and wags his tail." She leaned toward him. "So, Mr. Hardin, push my buttons and see what I'll do for you."

He smiled. "What was in that soda you had at the carnival?"

"Nothing. I'm just happy." She undid her seat belt and opened her door.

He slid out of the truck without a word and followed her. He used his key to unlock the back entrance, and then they were zooming up to the top floor. Holding her hand, he wondered if by some luck of the draw he'd found the perfect woman.

"This is my office," he said, unlocking his door.

"Do you have a secretary?"

"Not yet."

She winked. "Hire someone in her fifties. They're much better workers."

"Really?"

"Yes, I wouldn't lie," she said, deadpan. "Oh, my, look at this view." She gazed out the huge windows overlooking Houston.

When he was working, he barely noticed the view. He had other things on his mind. Looking at it with her, he saw how spectacular it was. Or maybe it was Shay. She was spectacular, too.

After locking his office again, he pointed to a door farther down. "That's my brother Cisco's office, or Kid, as we call him. The big door at the end is Cadde's. He's probably in there working, and I could introduce you, but he growls instead of talks, and we don't want to ruin our afternoon."

She playfully slapped his shoulder. "He does not."

"Maybe it just seems like it." He unlocked the door to the apartment, sincerely hoping

Cadde wasn't still in there. "Prepare your-self for pure gold-plated Roscoe." He swung open the door.

Shay stepped in and stopped, her eyes tak-ing in the lavish apartment, from the olive-green leather sofas facing each other to the Oriental rug, to the balcony and the view of Houston, to the paintings on the wall that cost more than she made in a year. This was wealth like she'd never seen before, and she felt out of place.

You're in over your head and you know it. Her mother's words were like a brain freeze, and Shay couldn't think beyond that. She couldn't think at all. All she knew was that she had to get out of here.

She backed toward the door. "I… I have to go…and get my car." In a second she was out the door and running for the elevator. As she pounded on the Down button she realized her car was at the dealership and her purse was in Chance's truck. She sank to the floor and wrapped her arms around her knees.

Stupid. Stupid. Stupid.

What a fool she'd made of herself.

But when she'd stepped into that apartment and saw how lavish it was, Shay had thought of her mother. The bottom line was always the money. Shay was different, wasn't she? The money didn't matter. She only wanted Chance. For a brief moment, though, she had to wonder if she was like her mother. The mere thought had sent her running.

She got to her feet before someone walked by and saw her. Now she had to go back into the apartment and apologize for making a fool of herself. She straightened her top and stiffened her backbone. Chance would understand. He would always understand, because he was that type of person—good to his soul.

Keep dreaming, Shay, she said to herself, and knocked on the door.

It opened immediately, as if Chance had been waiting for her to come back. Of course she had to. She had no wheels.

A worried frown creased his handsome face. "Are you okay?"

She shrugged. "Just feeling stupid."

"I'll get my keys and take you to your car."

"No." She stopped him.

"Shay." She could see he didn't believe her. "If you're uncomfortable…"

"I'm not," she assured him, and knew she had to tell him the truth. "When I saw this building, your office and this apartment, I realized you're the type of man my mother would date—a man with money."

"Whoa." He held up a hand. "I'm broke. I sank every dime I had into Shilah Oil."

"But with a promise of big dividends."

"Hopefully. It's a risk, like most things in life."

"The point is, for a brief moment, I wondered if a part of me is like my mother, and it spooked me. But as I sat by the elevator, trying to sort out my crazy thoughts, I realized the money means nothing. I want you. It's been that way since I first met you and you were a cowboy. I really liked that cowboy."

He gave a lopsided grin. "He's still here."

"And pushing all my buttons." She met his grin with one of her own.

He glanced at his watch. "We still have a little time before picking up the car."

"Please hold me," she said in a voice that sounded husky to her own ears.

His arms slipped around her waist and he kicked the door closed. He pulled her against his hard, firm body. As she breathed in his masculine scent and rested her face on his chest, she felt as if she'd found home, a place of warmth and love.

His hands moved up her back, caressing, probing almost.

"What are you doing?" she asked into the V of his shirt.

"Looking for that Try Me button."

Raising her head, she pointed to her lips.

"Ah," he breathed, and covered her mouth with his. The kiss went on and on as their tongues mingled and danced with new discoveries, new emotions. Almost without her knowing it her blouse and bra were gone. Her fingers undid the buttons of his shirt and she pressed into him, loving the feel of her breasts against his chest. He groaned and turned, half leading and half shuffling her down the hall. They stopped for a long heated kiss and then he drew her into the bedroom.

As he gently laid her down she had a glimpse of a large bed and antique furniture, but her attention was on Chance. He removed her heels, slacks and panties with ease, and almost at the same time removed his boots and jeans.

She gazed unashamedly at him. His body was perfectly shaped and muscled, his manhood very evident. "You're beautiful," she whispered.

"Ah, sweet Shay." His lips trailed from the

inside of her foot to her calf, to her thigh, and rested on her stomach. "You're the beautiful one. All soft and inviting. All woman." One hand went to the triangle between her legs while he lavished both breasts with his full attention. The world swayed and ebbed around her with shameless pleasure.

Her hands kneaded and stroked the muscles in his shoulders, his chest and lower. He groaned, catching her wrist.

"I'm on fire," he said against her lips, reaching for a condom on the nightstand.

"Me, too."

When he was fully sheathed he rolled onto her, and she welcomed him boldly, opening her legs. His lips found hers in a slow, drugged kiss as he thrust into her. She wrapped her arms and legs around him and held on for a ride that was better than any Ferris wheel.

A long time later their sweat-bathed bodies lay entwined. Shay kissed the swirls of hair on his chest, hating to end this moment. This time out of time when she'd found happiness with a man named Chance.

She eased from the bed, but he pulled her back. "Just one more minute."

"If we take a minute, it'll be ten and then twenty."

He tucked her long hair behind her ear. "You're amazing. It was amazing. Better than I'd even imagined in my dreams."

She kissed his hand and forced herself to stand. "I'll be smiling the rest of the day, and Darcy will want to know what's wrong with me."

"Nothing. Everything's right because... what are you doing?"

She ran her hand across the top of his foot. "These are some big feet." Her fingers trailed to his instep and he jerked, grinning.

"You're ticklish," she teased.

He yanked her back into bed and covered her naked body with his. "Nobody messes with my feet." A lopsided smile lifted the corners of his mouth.

"But me." She kissed him and he groaned.

"Yes, you...because—"

"Oh, Chance, look at the time. Where's my bra? My panties?" She jumped out of bed, stopping him. She was afraid he was going to say the words she feared—that he loved her. But she knew he did. She felt it in every touch, every kiss. He couldn't love a woman who kept secrets from him. Not until she told him the truth.

* * *

When Shay walked into her house, she could hear Darcy and Nettie.

"Stop jumping on the sofa," Nettie was saying. "If you don't, I'm going to turn you into a toad for good."

"Can you do that, Nettie? Can you really?"

"No, she can't," Shay said, placing her purse on the kitchen table. "And what are you doing, jumping on the sofa? You know you're not supposed to."

"Mom," Darcy shouted, and leapt down. "I was just showing Nettie how the sofa could be a trampoline."

"It's not," Shay reminded her.

Nettie got to her feet. "I'm going home to peace and quiet."

"Tell Nettie you're sorry for not minding her."

"Sorry," Darcy said, hugging Nettie around the waist and then turning to Shay. "Look." Her fingernails and toenails were purple. "Cool, huh?"

Before Shay could respond, the girl jumped up and down again. "Did you get us a car?"

"Yes, it's—"

Darcy screeched and ran to the garage.

Nettie searched Shay's face as if she were

reading her palm. "I'd say you spent the afternoon with a tall, dark stranger and enjoyed every minute."

Shay couldn't stop the smile that spread across her face. "Yes, I did."

Nettie hugged her. "Good for you." Then she drew back and pointed toward Blanche's room. "She's asked for you about four times in the last thirty minutes."

"I'll check on her." Shay headed for Blanche's room and then turned back. "Thanks for staying so long."

"Anytime. You know that."

"Love you." Shay hurried to her room and changed into jeans and a T-shirt. As she started to put her heels away, she noticed the dirt on them and remembered the carnival. She would always remember this day. A longing sigh escaped her. How she wished she could see Chance tonight. Wake up in his arms and...

"Shay!" Blanche called.

She made her way across the hall.

"Where in the hell have you been?"

Shay closed the door so Darcy couldn't hear. "Buying a car."

"You've been with a man," Blanche accused. "You've been with that Hardin boy."

"He's hardly a boy."

"I told you to break it off."

Shay ignored the warning. "Did you want something?"

"Yes. I want you to listen to me. He's trouble. Mark my words, you'll regret it."

"A few hours ago you wanted him to get your rings back."

"It's very clear you're not going to encourage that."

"No," Shay replied, trying not to lose her temper.

"He's no good to us then, so get rid of him." Blanche slapped a hand on the bed. "Go away. I spent thirty hours in labor and look what I got—a no-good daughter who won't even help me."

Shay backed out of the room and left her mother with her bitter thoughts. These little bouts of jealousy were hard on Shay. Her mom wanted to control her completely, but that wasn't happening.

When she reached the living room, she heard Darcy scream. *Oh, no.* Were the Bennett boys teasing her again? Shay hit the back door at a dead run, then stopped so fast she almost flipped.

Darcy had Chance by the hand and was

leading him toward the car. "This is our new car," she was telling him. "It's white," she added, as if Chance were color blind. She yanked open the passenger door. "This is where I sit. No one sits there but me and Tiny. Cool, huh?"

"Very cool, hotshot."

Darcy slammed the door. "Can I sit in your truck?"

"Sure."

Shay folded her arms across her chest. "The car has lost its appeal, huh?"

"No." Darcy made a face at her. "I can sit high up in Chance's truck. I can go through creeks, rivers, hills, mountains and all kinds of mud. I don't want to get our car dirty."

"Oh." In a child's mind pretend was what it was all about.

Darcy looked up at Chance. "Can I wear your hat?"

"Can I wear your hat, please?" Chance corrected her.

Darcy frowned. "I don't have a hat."

With a grin, Chance knelt down in front of her. "It's polite to say please when you want something. It's good manners."

"Oh." Darcy seemed to straighten her little frame. "Can I wear your hat, please?"

"Yes, you may," Chance replied, and plopped it on her head.

Darcy was out the door in a flash, Tiny on her heels.

"You're so good with her," Shay said, and moved into his arms, pressing against him and just loving the man he was.

He kissed the top of her head. "I couldn't stay in that apartment without you. I hope you don't mind me coming here."

She played with a button on his shirt. "Mind? I was trying to think of a way to get out tonight."

He leaned back, hope in his eyes. "Can you?"

"No." She took his hand and they walked into the house. "Is Darcy okay in your truck?"

"Yes, but I better go let the windows down so she doesn't suffocate."

Shay poked him in the chest. "That would be nice."

And so their evening went. They were together, that was the main thing. Darcy wanted pizza for supper, but Shay wanted her to have something healthy. Chance solved the problem by offering to pick up pizza and stop for a salad.

He looked at Darcy. "Would you like to go with me?"

Her head shot up. "You mean, like, in your truck? It's gonna be moving and everything?"

"I hope so." He smiled.

"Oh, wow. Golly gee, yes." Darcy ran for the door.

Chance kissed Shay. "I really hope we don't have to go through any rivers or creeks."

"Not with my kid," she called as he went out the door.

When they came back, Darcy's eyes were almost popping through her glasses with excitement. "Wow, Mom, you won't believe it," she said, placing the salad on the table. "You push a button and the window goes up and down. You push a button and the seat moves and you push a button and the air-conditioning gets cooler or hotter. And you push a button and the seat gets warm. Really, Mom. And I had my own control. How cool is that?"

"Supercool." Shay winked, taking the pizza from Chance.

"I like buttons," Darcy said, sliding into her seat.

"I like buttons, too." Chance looked at Shay's mouth and warmth suffused her whole body.

Almost in slow motion, she licked her quivering lips.

Chance walked past her to get to his chair. He patted her butt and whispered for her ears only, "Stop teasing."

She giggled and they sat down to eat—like a real family.

That phrase lingered in her mind. That's what she wanted—a real loving family. It was a fantasy, though. She knew a fallout was coming and she had to be prepared. For now she was selfishly clinging to her secret, clinging to Chance. The truth would only hurt him and she was trying to protect him from the pain.

Would he understand that?

Chapter Eleven

Before Chance knew it, June had arrived but he hardly noticed. He was happier than he'd even been, and it was all because of Shay. She'd reached his heart when no one else could. At times he found it hard to keep his mind on business. But he managed. Since the weather was nicer, the rigs were drilling.

He'd taken the helicopter in for service and it was being delivered back today. Then he'd be off for the Giddings field. He cleared up his paperwork and left notes for Cadde and Kid on the Crocker Number One well. The geologist predicted this would be their biggest producer so far. Cadde wanted it watched closely.

But Chance drew the line at working late. He usually landed on the roof about five, showered, changed and was at Shay's by six. No way was he giving up time with her, especially Tuesday and Thursday nights, when she came to the apartment after her classes at the University of Houston. Cadde could yell all he wanted, but Chance wasn't clocking in twelve to fourteen hour days.

He had other interests besides the oil business.

His main interest was a green-eyed lady named Shay.

As he was about to leave, his phone buzzed. He picked up the receiver. He really needed to hire a secretary.

"Yes," he said into the receiver.

"Mr. Hardin." The receptionist's sugary voice came on the line. "There's a Mrs. Renee Calhoun here to see you. What do you want me to do?"

"Send her up," he replied, wondering what Renee was doing in Houston.

He opened the outer door and ushered Renee in. She looked elegant, as always, in a beige designer suit and pearls.

As she took a seat, he asked, "What's up?"

She sat her purse on the floor. "I came to ask a favor."

"Fire away." He leaned back in his chair. "I'm pretty easy."

"You're a very nice young man. I miss you at the ranch." She looked around the office. "Your new venture seems to be going well."

"So far so good." He paused. "So what's the favor?"

Renee reached for her Louis Vuitton bag and rifled through it. She pulled out a black velvet ring box and placed it on his desk. He'd seen that box before. Blanche's rings. This was a puzzling development.

"Could you please give those to Shay?"

He looked at the older woman's face and saw nothing but peace there. "I thought you'd never change your mind. You were very angry."

She folded her hands in her lap. "Sorry you had to witness that."

"It was a normal reaction."

"It was a jealous reaction," she corrected. "But I got over it."

"What changed your mind?"

"When I heard that Shay was not Jack's biological daughter, something shifted in me and I could see my behavior for what it was—pure jealousy." She waved a hand toward the box. "Those are Blanche's rings and she should have them. I know what a wedding ring means to a woman. Besides, I really don't want to keep them in the house any longer."

"That's very generous and forgiving."

She rose to her feet. "What can I say? I'm a saint."

Chance stood, too. "Can I ask you a favor in return?"

She slipped the purse over her arm. "Sure."

He pushed the rings toward her. "Would you please give these to Shay yourself?"

"Oh, Chance." Clearly that was something she didn't want to do.

"She feels bad about trying to steal them, and if you two met again I think it would close that door on the past forever."

Renee picked up the rings. "For you I'll do it, but I really would rather not see Blanche."

"Don't worry. She never leaves her bedroom." He quickly scribbled directions on a piece on paper. "The house is easy to find and it's on your way out of town."

Chance walked around his desk and handed it to her. "Thank you."

"Yeah. That's the problem with being a saint. You're an easy target." She headed for the door.

"Renee." Chance didn't know how to phrase his question. He didn't even know why he wanted to ask it, but it was there at the front of his mind, urging him on. He had to know.

"Yes." She looked at him.

"May I ask you a personal question?"

"Depends how personal."

"No." He shook his head. "It's not about you. It's about me."

"Oh, well then, ask away."

Chance took a long breath. "Did you ever see my father with another woman?"

"Heavens no. He was devoted to your mother."

Chance watched her face. "You said that a little too fast."

Her skin paled. "Chance, I don't know anything."

But she did. High Cotton was a small town and gossip was rampant. "What do you know?"

"Nothing, really." She slipped her purse higher on her arm. "Your mother came to the ranch collecting donations to send the basket-

ball team to state. She came in, we had coffee and talked."

"And?"

"We got to talking about men and relation-
ships. She said she'd loved Chuck since high
school and there would never be anyone else
for her. But she added that lately Chuck had
been distant and working a lot of overtime.
I think she suspected he was seeing someone else."

"He was," Chance said. "I just don't know
who."

"Chance." Renee touched his arm. "Let it
go. It's been over twenty years. Let them rest
in peace. It's time to live your own life. Take
that from a woman who knows."

"I'll try," he promised.

She hugged him. "I think you've found
someone to help you. Am I right?"

He tried to hide a smile, but couldn't. "Yes,
I'm seeing Shay. She's a wonderful person,
just like we thought from the start."

"Trust those first instincts. They're almost
always right." Renee reached for the door-
knob. "Now I have a delivery to make. Goodbye, Chance."

"Bye," he called, and fumbled for the phone

on his leather belt. Shay answered immediately.

"Renee Calhoun is coming your way," he said. "I just wanted to give you a heads-up."

"What? Chance, why is she coming here?"

"Relax and trust me."

"Chance..." He clicked off and headed for the helicopter pad, ignoring his ringing phone. He hoped she trusted him enough to know that he wouldn't send Renee over there with murder in her eye.

No way would he let anyone hurt Shay.

She was the one thing in his world that was rock-solid good and he intended to hold on until the last turn of the Ferris wheel.

Shay was so nervous she could barely finish Mrs. Willet's hair. What did Renee want with her? Chance had said to relax and trust him, and she found that was all she could do.

Mrs. Willet paid for her services and walked to the door. "My, there's a big old Cadillac driving up."

Mrs. Taylor jumped out of Nettie's chair to look. "Wonder if she's lost?"

"I'll take care of it," Shay said, and removed her smock.

Darcy joined Mrs. Taylor at the window.

"Golly, she looks like a fairy godmother."
School was out, so Darcy had to go to work
with Shay and sometimes she grew bored. "I
want to go."

With her hand on the door, she said, "No.
You stay here with Nettie."

"I wanna come," Darcy wailed.

"Read your book. I won't be long."

"No," Darcy snapped in anger.

Nettie came to Shay's aid. "If you don't
mind your mother, I'm going to turn you into
a big fat toad."

Darcy whirled around. "You don't know
how to do that."

Before Shay could intervene, Nettie flung
out her arms. In the gypsy blouse she looked
like a bird about to take flight. "Abracadabra,
saints and sinners, doubters and believers…"

Darcy scurried to her chair and buried her
face in her book, peering over the top at Nettie.

Nettie lowered her arms and winked
at Shay. Those made-up incantations had
worked on Shay as a child and still seemed
to be potent—at least to a little girl.

Shay opened the door and went out to meet
Renee, who stood by the Cadillac looking elegant and sophisticated.

"I'm sorry," was all Shay could say.

Renee waved a hand, her diamond rings flashing. "Don't worry about it, sugar. I know Blanche and how she can manipulate people."

"Still, it was wrong, and I should never have—"

"I could write a book about the 'never haves' in my life, so let's just leave it in the past where it should be."

"You're so gracious—not at all like the woman I'd heard about for so many years."

Renee lifted a fine arched eyebrow. "The bitch, huh?"

Shay nodded.

"That works both ways, sugar. Blanche and I used to be friends, two young girls from poor families looking for a better way of life. We just happened to fall in love with the wrong man."

"Jack Calhoun," Shay murmured. "If I never hear his name again, I'll be happy. For so many years I believed he was my father." She looked down at her hands, and the scent of permanent solution wafted to her, reminding her of who she really was. "I have to be honest. The main reason my mother was able to talk me into going to Southern Cross was that I thought I had…a right…a right as

Jack's daughter to be there. When I saw how beautiful the place was, I felt cheated out of so much…but it was all a lie. My life was a lie…"

"Oh, sugar." Renee hugged her, and the scent of Chanel replaced the putrid permanent solution. "Blanche needs to be horse-whipped."

"I think God took care of that." She brushed away an errant tear.

"How is Blanche?"

"Not good. Breathing is very difficult for her and she's confined to her room now."

"Do you take care of her?"

"Yes, with the aid of Home Health."

"Blanche is lucky to have you. Most daughters would have put her butt in a home by now."

Shay wiped her hands on the back of her jeans. "I thought about it, but couldn't."

Renee touched her cheek lightly. "Chance said our first instincts about you were right. You're a very nice young lady."

"Thank you," she said, and felt herself stand a little taller.

"And speaking of Chance, I have something to give you." Renee reached into the car. "He thought it would be better if I gave this to you instead of to him." Renee pulled out a ring box and Shay gasped, taking a step backward.

"No, no." She shook her head. "If those are Mom's rings, I can't accept them."

"Well, sugar, we have a problem then." Renee glanced down at the box in her hand. "I thought hell would freeze over or the Cowboys would win the Super Bowl before I'd offer these rings to her. But Jack bought them for her and she should have them. Just tossing them away would be destructive, and I'm not a destructive person. As Chance put it so gallantly, a person should be granted her dying wish." Renee reached for Shay's hand and placed the box in her palm. "Do what you want with them."

"This is so generous, so forgiving."

"As I told Chance, I'm a saint." She laughed lightly and got into her car.

"Thank you," Shay called.

Renee poked her head out the window. "One more thing, Shay. Don't break Chance's heart. He's too nice of a guy for that."

"Yes, he is," she whispered as she watched Renee back out of the driveway. With the rings clasped in her hand, she walked toward the shop.

Don't break Chance's heart rang through her head like an alarm she couldn't turn off. There was no *don't*. It was *when* she'd break his heart.

It was just a matter of time.

At lunch Shay fixed tomato soup and a grilled cheese sandwich for Darcy and a pro-tein smoothie for Blanche. The Home Health lady said she couldn't get Blanche to eat, so Shay thought she might like something easy on her stomach.

"Lunch," she said, entering her room.

"Go away," her mother retorted, and turned onto her side.

"I have a surprise for you, but you can't have it until you drink some of the smoothie."

"A surprise?" She turned over, eager as a child for a toy.

"You have to sit up."

"Oh, Shay."

"Come on." She helped Blanche into a sit-ting position and handed her the drink, while clutching the ring box in her left hand.

Blanche sipped at the smoothie.

"More," Shay urged.

When it was half-gone, Blanche said, "I can't drink any more."

Shay took the glass from her and placed it on the nightstand. Then she opened her hand.

Blanche's eyes opened wide and she glanced from Shay's hand to her face. "Oh, oh, those are my rings."

"Yes," Shay replied.

Blanche grabbed the box and opened it. She gaped at the rings for a second, then removed them. Her hand shook as she slipped them onto her finger.

"They're too big," she cried.

"You've lost a lot of weight. I'll get some tape."

A few minutes later Blanche lay back in the bed, gazing lovingly at her rings. She looked ten years younger. Shay thought it strange that a material thing could bring her so much joy.

"How did you get them?" Blanche finally asked.

"I didn't. Renee brought them."

"That bitch."

"No," Shay corrected. "That very nice lady. She didn't have to give you the rings, but out of the goodness of her heart she did."

Blanche ignored her words, holding up her hand, the light catching the sparkle of the diamonds. "Jack is happy I have my rings. I was the love of his life."

"Renee was the love of his life. You ripped them apart briefly, but he married her again and they were a family until his death."

"Hand me the album," Blanche demanded, shutting out everything Shay was saying.

There was no thank-you. Nothing. But that was Blanche and her sense of entitlement.

Shay placed the album on the bed and left her mother to her world of make-believe.

Shay didn't book anyone after four because Chance sometimes came early and she wanted to spend that time with him.

Darcy was restless and followed her from room to room. "When is Chance coming?"

"When he gets off work." Shay stuffed clothes into the washing machine.

The change that Chance had made in Darcy was amazing. She'd never had a father figure in her life before, and she looked up to him and respected him. *Please* was now one of her favorite words and she used it sometimes when she didn't need to, not wanting to disappoint him. Every day it was the same old question: "When is Chance coming?"

"Oh, oh." Darcy made a dash for the front door. "I hear Chance's truck. He's here."

Shay checked the roast in the Crock-Pot, letting Darcy have this time with Chance. He strolled into the kitchen, Darcy in one arm and a bag in his other hand. Shay's heart knocked against her ribs at the gleam in his eyes.

"What do you have there?"

"Besides Darcy, I have ice cream." He held up the bag.

"What kind?"

"Blue Bell Rocky Road."

She licked her lips. "I love chocolate."

"Me, too." Darcy didn't want to be left out. "May I sit in your truck, please?"

"Sure thing, hotshot." He lowered Darcy to the floor. "The windows are already down."

Shay went into his arms and kissed him slowly, savoring the taste and feel of him. "Thank you," she whispered.

"If ice cream has this effect on you, I'll bring it every night."

She poked him in the chest. "It's not about the ice cream, which by the way is very cold on my butt."

With a grin, he released her and put the ice cream in the freezer.

"I was talking about the rings," she said when he turned around.

"I had nothing to do with that. That was Renee's idea."

"You sent her here, though, and it was good to talk to her—to apologize."

"I'm glad." He leaned against the cabinet. "Was Blanche happy?"

"Ecstatic."

"I'd like to meet her. Maybe after supper."

Shay's hand shook as she reached for plates. "She doesn't like people to see her the way she is." Shay cringed at the partial white lie. Blanche didn't like people to see her faded beauty, but she'd jump at the opportunity to talk to Chance—only to hurt him.

"Oh. I wouldn't want to make her uncomfortable."

There was hurt in his voice and Shay couldn't stand it. She put the plates down and leaned against him, playing with his shirt buttons. "Meeting my mother would not be a pleasant experience. She's everything you've ever heard about her, and I won't have her hurting your feelings. You'll have to settle for Darcy and me."

He wasn't satisfied, though. "Does she hurt your feelings?"

"All the time, but I'm her daughter."

"Still…"

"She's in the last stages of lung cancer and she's bitter and angry. I try to remember that."

He opened his legs to pull Shay tight against him. She pressed into every hard angle. "You're amazing," he whispered into her mouth.

The kiss was long and drugging. The slamming of the front door had them breaking apart.

Darcy chatted nonstop through supper. She wanted Chance to know everything she did and everything that crossed her child mind. Shay thought she was going to have to tape her mouth shut.

"Whoa, hotshot." Chance finally made a time-out sign. "My head is spinning and I'm not sure I believe that fairy godmother story." He carried his plate to the sink.

Darcy followed him. "She was here, Chance, but Mommy wouldn't let me talk to her."

He leaned back against the cabinet, his arms folded across his chest. "What would you say to her?"

"Fairy godmothers grant wishes, right?"

"I suppose." He bent down, his hands on

his knees. "You have a wish you wanted to ask her?"

Darcy's head bobbed like a cork.

"What was it?"

She twisted her hands. "I can't tell you. It won't come true."

"It's just between you and me."

"Well." Darcy's voice dropped low so Shay couldn't hear, but she heard every word. "My mommy needs a husband and I need a daddy."

"Oh." Clearly, Chance was shocked by the wish. "Do you have someone in mind?"

Darcy nodded vigorously.

"Who?"

"No. No. No! I can't tell." She went screeching into the living room.

Blanche was going to love that. But it was Darcy's home, too.

Shay looked up and caught the gleam in Chance's dark eyes. He knew who Darcy was talking about.

So did she.

And it made it that much harder to do what she had to.

Chapter Twelve

Chance declared that he and Darcy would do the dishes. Shay had worked all day and cooked supper, so she needed to put her feet up.

If she had been granted a wish to conjure up the perfect man, he would be just like Chance. He was absolutely perfect in every way. She didn't understand why fate had thrown them together, only to tear them apart.

The ringing of the phone interrupted her thoughts. "I'll get it," she called, "since I'm not allowed in the kitchen."

She saw the caller ID and frowned. What did Sally want?

"Shay, I'm sorry." Petey's mom rushed into speech. "I shouldn't have said what I did about Darcy. I was just upset."

"And you need a babysitter." Shay took the portable phone and walked into the living room.

Sally ignored her words. "Petey can get into enough trouble on his own. I don't know why I was blaming Darcy. I guess to keep from blaming myself. It's hard raising three kids alone. I'm an awful mother. I never seem to get anything right."

The hard stance Shay had been planning to take vanished. She knew what Sally was going through. She went through it every day herself.

"And, yes, I need a babysitter," Sally added. "The restaurant I work at on weekends called to see if I could work the bar. The tips are great and I need the money. My daughter has a date and my older son is off with his friends. I don't have anywhere to leave Petey."

"Send him over," Shay said without hesitation. "Please pick him up by ten."

There was a long pause on the line. "I have to work till twelve or later, but my daughter will pick him up."

"Ten, Sally. No later." This time Shay wasn't going to let Sally take advantage of her.

"Okay. I'll bring him."

Shay went back to the kitchen and put the phone on the hook. There was a knock at the door. Could that be Petey? Sally must have been outside with her cell. Shay shook her head. She was such a patsy.

"Darcy, get the door, please."

"Ah, Mom, I'm helping Chance."

"Your mother asked you to get the door," Chance said in a voice that brooked no arguments.

"Okay." And just like that Darcy darted off to the door. Shay could use some of that magic.

"Petey," Darcy screeched. "Mom, it's Petey."

"My mom said I could play with you for a while."

"I got company."

"Who?" Petey asked.

"Chance." Obviously Darcy thought he came to see her.

"The guy with the truck?"

"Yep. Maybe he'll play ball with us." The two ran into the kitchen to ask him.

"Oh, how nice it is to be popular." Chance

kissed Shay's cheek and followed the kids out the back door.

Shay sighed and prepared her mom some soup for supper. Blanche still ate very little, but was in a better mood because of the rings. Shay straightened the bed and settled her in for the night.

To get the beauty shop smell from her clothes, Shay decided to take a shower. Afterward she slipped into shorts and a tank top, feeling much cooler and refreshed. On her way to get the clothes out of the dryer, she stopped short in the living room and peered through the double windows.

Chance was playing ball with the kids— not only with Darcy and Petey, but Bruce and Michael, too. What were the Bennetts doing here? They seemed friendly. The group was in a circle and they were throwing the ball to each other. Chance threw to Bruce, who quickly caught the ball and immediately threw it to Darcy, who threw to Michael, who threw to Petey. And on it went. The circle got bigger after each round of throws. She supposed it was a game, because when Petey missed the ball, he sat on the grass and watched. Finally there was just Chance and Bruce left. Bruce tried to throw it over

Chance's head and failed. Chance caught it every time. Didn't the boy know he wasn't getting a thing over that long, tall Texan's head?

Finally, Bruce missed and he fell down on the ground, but he wasn't mad. He was smiling. The boy got up and went over to Chance. They were talking, obviously about baseball.

Darcy leaned on Chance, wanting the boys to know he was her friend, not theirs. It grew dark and Chance, Darcy and Petey made their way inside. Chance dished ice cream into bowls for everyone.

"Mom, I forgave the Bennetts for busting my lip," Darcy said, spooning ice cream into her mouth.

"You did?"

"Yeah. They were hiding in the bushes, watching us, and Chance said we should invite them to play. I said no. They're mean."

She swallowed a mouthful of ice cream. "But Chance said good people forgive. I'm a good people, so I forgave them and they said they were sorry, too."

Shay stared at Chance. "Wow. I'd call that a Chance miracle."

"Yeah, Mom, he's good at that."

"He's good at a lot of things," she said with a lifted eyebrow.

"Later I'll show you how good," he whispered in her ear as he passed her to put his bowl in the sink.

She giggled like an impressionable teenager and realized how wonderful it was just to have fun.

As Darcy and Petey fell down in front of the TV, a car honked outside.

"Petey, your sister is here."

"Gotta go." He ran for the door.

Shay looked outside to make sure it was Petey's sister, then walked back into the living room and saw Darcy almost asleep on the floor.

"Bathtime, sweetie."

"Ah, Mom. It's summer and I'm tired."

Shay expected Chance to say something, but he didn't. At that moment she realized she was leaning on him too much. She had to stop that. She reached down and took Darcy's hand, lifting her to her feet, then marched her into the bathroom. Since her child was practically asleep, Shay bathed her. She didn't want her to drown in the tub.

Wrapping a big towel around Darcy's body, Shay thought how thin she was. But the doctor said it was nothing to worry about. Darcy had a lot of excessive energy—Shay just had to make sure she ate a healthy diet. Like Sally, Shay wasn't sure she was doing all the right things. Motherhood was trial and error, she found.

As she tucked her in, Darcy mumbled, "Bruce thought he could beat Chance. No way. Then Bruce wanted throwing tips. Gotta make it burn, Mommy. That's what Chance says. Gotta make it burn."

Shay kissed her forehead, smiling. Chance had all the kids enthralled—including her.

She walked back into the living room and stopped in the doorway. The room was in darkness except for the light streaming from the kitchen. Soft music from the TV played in the background. Her heart pounded in anticipation.

Chance sat on the sofa and she walked over to him, straddling his lap and pressing her breasts against his chest.

"Ah." He kissed the side of her face while removing the clip from her hair. "I've been waiting for this all day." His hands trailed through her long tresses.

"Me, too," she whispered against his lips.

"I like these." He tugged at the hem of her

shorts. "And I love this." His hand slid over her thigh. "Actually, I love everything about you."

"Even my daughter."

"Even your daughter."

Shay slowly unbuttoned his shirt. "You're a special man, and sometimes I think you can't be real and that you're going to disappear in a puff of smoke."

"I'm not going anywhere." His hands slid under her tank top to her breasts. "Oh, no, I'm not going anywhere."

At his kiss, his touch, her brain shut down and she went with the feelings that were surging through her—warm erotic feelings he created in her. His lips took hers in a burst of need. She pressed closer, needing to feel his skin against hers. The kiss went on and on until thinking was a problem.

"Whoa." Chance eased his lips to her cheek. "I see a red light coming, and if we don't stop there won't be enough cold water in this town to help me."

"Chance." She buried her face in his neck.

He stroked her hair. "Do you know how much I love you?"

Shay froze and moved away from him to sit on the sofa.

"What's wrong?" She could feel his startled eyes on her.

Desperate words flew from her mouth. "You can't love me. You can't love me."

"What?" He sat up straight.

The fallout was here, and she should run for cover, for shelter. But she could do nothing but accept the inevitable.

"I told you from the start that I couldn't get involved. It's too complicated. I have a kid…"

Chance stiffened. "That's bull. Tell me what's really wrong."

She swallowed the wad of cowardice in her throat and forced the words out. "I don't love you." They tasted bitter on her tongue and she had the urge to throw up.

He stared at her, and even though she couldn't see his eyes clearly, she knew he was stunned, angry even.

"So…these past few weeks…what has that been about? Was it just sex for you?"

Her throat locked in pain and she couldn't speak. How did she explain? With the truth, maybe? But it was buried so deep she couldn't bring it up.

"Was it?" he demanded.

"Yes," she lied, and felt the ache of that lie sear through her.

Tense silence ate up time.

"You're lying," he finally said. "It was more than sex. You know that. I know that."

"Chance." She stood and stepped away from him. His pain was a tangible thing she could feel. "My mother dated a lot of men and used them to get what she wanted. She never loved them. I don't want to be like her."

He jammed a hand through his hair and buttoned his shirt. "You're not like that."

The words were in her throat and she had to say them again. "I don't love you." She hated hurting him like this. Ending it now was best for both of them, though. She should never have gone on that first date. Even so, she should have had enough sense to end it long ago, but she'd selfishly hung on to him, knowing full well there was no future.

He reached for his hat on the coffee table. "I don't know what's going on here but…"

"Please. I want you to leave."

"Does love scare you that much?" he asked, and she knew he wasn't giving up easily.

"Chance… I…"

"Okay." The entreaty in her voice must have gotten to him. "If you want me to go, I will, but I know something's not right. Maybe one day you'll have the courage to tell me what that is." Swinging around, he headed for the door.

"Chance."

The door slammed shut and then she heard the squeal of tires on the pavement. He was gone—for good this time. Her stomach cramped and she wrapped her arms around her waist. Why did she have to fall in love with the one man she couldn't have? When he found out the truth, he would hate her. But all the pain he was experiencing now would vanish, and he would be glad he wasn't involved with her.

She sank to the floor, pulled up her knees and buried her face on them. *Don't break Chance's heart.* Renee's words came back to her like a dart through her heart. But it wasn't over yet. There was still more pain to come.

"I love you, Chance," Shay murmured, bracing herself for a future without him.

Chance drove and drove, unable to go home to a lonely apartment. But no matter how far he traveled he couldn't outrun her words. *I don't love you.* Had he misread the signs? Was the relationship all on his side? He didn't think so, though that just might be his ego talking. Rejection burned like a rope across his skin.

In a matter of a few minutes his world had shattered, much as it had twenty-two years ago. He'd survived that, and would survive this. He wished he understood why, though.

He'd called a Realtor and told her what he was looking for—a big house with acreage. He wanted to have horses, so Darcy could learn to ride, and he wanted to get them out of that crappy neighborhood. His whole world centered around Shay and Darcy. He couldn't wait to get off work to be with them. They made him happy. They eased the pain of the past. And now…now it was over. A pain gripped his chest. Why?

He looked up and realized he was on the Katy Freeway going nowhere. Turning the truck around, he headed back to Houston and his apartment.

But he still didn't understand why.

Chance planned to work nonstop. At least Cadde would be happy. That was the only way to put the pain behind him. He was in his office early, mapping out his route for the day. They had a rig in the repair shop and he had to check on that.

Kid breezed in. "Hey, you working today? It's Sunday."

"Yep. I'm working."

Kid sat on the edge of Chance's desk. "Why aren't you with the girlfriend?"

"We broke up." Chance looked at his brother. "Or more to the point, she broke up with me. Evidently she's not into a serious relationship."

"You're kidding. Every woman I've ever dated has wanted the ring, marriage and babies—the whole chain-around-the-neck thing."

"Shay's not like that," he said quickly, and then caught himself. He didn't really know her, so he couldn't say. He knew her body, though, every soft curve, every sensitive spot that made her moan, and her Try Me button was—

"Mind if I call her?" Kid flopped into a chair. "Sounds like the perfect woman."

"Yes, I mind if you call her," Chance replied, his voice heavy with umbrage. "Leave Shay alone."

"Damn." Kid snapped his fingers. "Sounds as if you're not over her."

He decided not to answer that. "What are you doing in the office this morning?"

"Date last night didn't go the way I'd planned, so I thought I'd get some work done."

"You wanted hot sex and she didn't?"

"Something like that."

Chance closed the folder he was writing in. "Are you ever going to grow up?"

"Lordy, I hope not. Life's too much fun this way." Kid propped his boots on Chance's desk.

Chance just shook his head. "Well, I'm off to…" His cell phone beeped and he hurriedly picked it up, hoping it was Shay. It wasn't.

"Hey, Sam." Sam was the tool pusher on Crocker Number One. "What's up?"

"We broke a pipe."

"Damn it. Start pulling the pipe out. I'm on my way."

"What happened?" Kid asked. Chance told him.

"Man, Cadde's going to be pissed."

"I know." Chance picked up his hard hat. "I'm on my way to tell him, and then I'm heading to the well."

"I'll change boots, grab my hard hat and go with you."

"Okay." Chance headed down the hall. "Do you think Cadde's in?"

Kid laughed. "Hell, yeah."

"Son of a bitch," Cadde muttered when he heard the news. "I'll get my boots and hat and go with you. I want to see firsthand what's going on."

"I can take care of it," Chance said.

"But three Hardins can take care of it faster."

Within minutes they were in the helicopter and headed for Crocker Number One. Chance landed the aircraft smoothly some distance from the well. Sam's eyes opened wide when he saw all three brothers get off the chopper.

"It's all under control, sir." Sam spoke to Cadde. "We're trying to reach the broken pipe."

Chance looked up to see roughnecks busy on the platform, attaching chains and ropes to a pipe as a large hydraulic lift hoisted it up out of the well. A man high on the derrick looped a rope around it and roughnecks guided it to the pipe rack. They repeated the process as mud, grime and oil coated the drilling platform.

"I'll see for myself," Cadde said, turning to Sam. "I need work gloves." Sam immediately found three pairs. Slipping his on, Cadde headed for the platform. Chance and

Kid exchanged glances and followed, shoving their own hands into gloves.

"Going smoothly, sir," Mick, the driller, shouted above the roar of the rig.

Suddenly mud that kept the drilling process cool spewed up from the well, splattering everyone on the platform. No one winced or said a word. If you were a roughneck, you were used to the muck and grime of drilling.

"I want this well back on track," Cadde said, as if nothing had happened.

"Yes, sir. We're doing our best."

Just then a loud bang cut through the noise of the rig. Chance looked up to see Brad, the derrick man, hanging in thin air. His safety harness held him in place.

"Shut down the rig," Cadde ordered. Chance knew how hard that was for him, but a man's life was at stake.

Several roughnecks shouted up to Brad, but he didn't move.

"Something's wrong," Cadde said. "I'm going up to see if I can attach his harness to a pulley line that will bring him down. Any other suggestions?"

"I can climb the derrick," Chance offered.

Cadde ignored the suggestion. "You and

Kid be ready to catch him when he slides down."

They watched as Cadde climbed the derrick. Once he reached the crow's nest, as Brad's position was called, he caught the safety cables that were attached to the derrick. Using them, he slowly pulled Brad toward him, and then reached for the pulley line the derrick man used every day to slide down after work.

Evidently Brad was deadweight, because Cadde was having a hell of a time attaching his harness to the pulley. Finally he waved a hand. "He's coming down," he called on the Sunday morning breeze.

Chance, Kid and four roughnecks hurried down the platform to catch Brad. He came down fast, but Chance made sure he landed smoothly, just as an ambulance roared onto the site.

A paramedic quickly checked Brad, who was lying on the grass, lifeless.

"I'm not getting a response," he said. "Let's get him to a hospital. Go, go, go!"

Brad was pasty and pale, and Chance worried he was dead. Probably a heart attack, but he was so young—only twenty-four, with a young wife. This part of the oil business sucked. This part of life sucked.

He heard a shout and turned to see Cadde slipping off the derrick into the ropes, chains and pulleys. His hard hat plummeted, bouncing off the platform moments later, as Cadde hung there like a broken kite. A chain held his right boot, and that was the only thing keeping him from tumbling to his death, headfirst.

For a split second Chance couldn't move.

A scream shattered his shock. It was Kid. Roughnecks tried to hold him back from the derrick, but Kid broke free.

Chance realized he was already on the derrick, climbing up to save his brother.

Not another death in his family, he vowed, climbing higher.

Not another death.

Chapter Thirteen

Chance reached their brother first. "Cadde," he called, but Cadde was unmoving. His right boot was being held by a rope, not a chain, he noted. His left foot lay against a pipe they had pulled out of the well.

"Cadde," Kid yelled in turn, and again there was not a flicker of response. After surveying the position of Cadde's body, Kid looked up at Chance. "How do we get him out of here? We can't use the pulley, 'cause he's inside the derrick wall." Kid glanced around. "Where's the crane?"

"It's on another job." Chance had already thought of that, but the crane was too far away. They needed to get Cadde down now as safely and quickly as possible.

A warm June breeze cooled Chance's sweaty body as he held on to the derrick. He viewed the situation again and knew they had to stabilize Cadde before he catapulted downward. At the moment that had to be their main goal. "I'm going to try to tie his legs together and secure him to the derrick."

"But..."

"The rope could give at any minute, Kid. We don't have many choices."

"Sir."

Chance looked down to see Woody, one of the roughnecks, with a rope over his shoulder. Two other roughnecks were there with ropes. He hadn't even noticed them.

Very carefully, he reached for Cadde's left foot. If he missed...if he jarred it in any way...the pipe, ropes and chains could all crash downward. Holding his breath, he stretched as far as he could with his right arm and closed his hand on a fistful of denim. Once he had a good grip, Woody handed him the rope. Chance looped it around both legs with one hand, and was amazed to find he hadn't forgotten a thing from his days of hog-tying steers.

He secured Cadde to the derrick, then let out a long, agonizing breath. Now his brother would not tumble to his death. But they still had to get him down.

"We have to secure his arms," Chance shouted to Kid. Woody and Mick scurried to help, as did Chance. "Okay. Here's what we do. I'm going to pull him in as close as I can. Woody and Mick, your jobs are to get his arms up so Kid can secure them to his chest. Ready?"

"His head is bleeding," Kid said. "We have to do this quickly."

"No," Chance told him. "We have to do this carefully. Concentrate. Focus. Let's do it." He held on to the derrick with one hand and reached out with his other for his brother. The first attempt failed, and Chance swore under his breath as the Texas sun bored through his hard hat. He took a sharp breath and noted the quiet. Around an oil rig there was always noise. But not today. The crew on the ground was looking up in silence. No roar of the rig, no pipes or chains rattling, no yelling—just silence. Dead silence.

"Everyone ready?" he called as he attempted another try.

"Yes," echoed through the stillness.

Again Chance stretched out his arm, straining toward his brother with everything in him. This time he was able to shove two fingers into Cadde's waistband and pull. Woody and Mick went into action, each lifting an arm upward to Cadde's side. Holding on with one arm, Kid threw the rope and jerked it tight around Cadde's chest. They had him hog-tied.

And safe. For now.

"Is he breathing?" Kid asked.

"I can't tell," Chance replied, not letting his mind go in that direction. He had to concentrate. Stay focused.

He turned to Woody. "Tell Sam to send up the medical cage, more ropes and some bandages."

"Yes, sir." Woody scurried down like a monkey.

"How in the hell are we going to get him in the cage?" Kid wanted to know.

"With brute strength," Chance replied. And little else.

He looked toward the sky and saw the Texas and U.S. flags waving in the breeze at the top of the derrick. For a moment, all he could see were green eyes. They disappeared in a haze of thundercloud blue as the sun disappeared. He could use some of Nettie's magic right about now. But the only kind of magic he knew, the only kind his mother had taught him, was the real deal. His eyes centered on the rolling clouds and he prayed like he'd never prayed before.

Woody returned with a rope wrapped around each shoulder and a bandage in his pocket. He pulled out the latter and handed it to Kid. "Mr. Sam said to peel off the back and stick it on."

Kid followed instructions and leaned out to apply it. "It's soaking up the blood."

"Maybe it will clot," Chance said, as two roughnecks inched upward with the medical cage. "Apply some pressure."

"It's not working," Kid yelled in a frantic voice. "We have to get him to a hospital."

"Calm down," Chance shouted. He had one brother in crisis. He didn't need another.

The stretcher with the leather straps reached them. "What's the plan?" Kid asked.

"We have to get his body on it." Chance glanced toward the threatening sky and felt a warm gust of wind on his face. "We could use a little help," he whispered. Almost on request, the dark clouds vanished and the sun poked through again, bathing them in sunshine. *"Thank you,"* he mouthed, and devised a plan to save his brother.

He didn't have to do much planning. The roughnecks, who'd faced many crises on the rigs, knew what to do. They were hardworking men devoted to a dangerous job. And right now they were all devoted to saving their boss.

Four roughnecks with two-by-fours tucked against their bodies climbed the derrick from the other side. Chance knew what they were going to do. He didn't need to tell them. With the two-by-fours they were going to guide the stretcher down and keep it from jarring against the derrick.

Now they had to get Cadde on it.

Woody and Mick aligned the stretcher against Cadde's long body. The other roughnecks held it in place with the two-by-fours. Chance and Kid went to work strapping Cadde into the cage with the attached leather thongs. Then Chance looped a rope around and around their brother, making sure Cadde was firmly anchored inside the cage.

Kid positioned Cadde's head in the padded horseshoe-shaped headrest and tightened a strap across his forehead.

They both worked while holding on to the

derrick with one hand, and using the other to the best of their ability.

"We got him secure," Kid finally called.

Chance shoved his hand into the carrying handle so he could use his arm to take the weight off Kid's back.

Kid did the same for more leverage.

Woody and Mick climbed to stand between them, each with a grip on the stretcher. The other roughnecks were in place with the two-by-fours.

They were ready.

"Okay, boys," Chance shouted. "Let's go down—slowly. Wait a minute." He realized they had one small problem. Cadde was still anchored to the derrick.

"I'll get it, sir," Woody called, realizing the problem at the same time. He crawled higher and reached up to undo Cadde's legs.

Chance felt the weight on his arm, and his muscles tightened. But he held on.

Woody then hurried down to release Cadde's chest. "Ready," he called.

"Let it go," Kid said, and Chance knew Kid was bracing for the weight that was about to come down on him.

Slowly, Woody untied the knot and Cadde was deadweight in their hands. Kid groaned under the impact. Chance pulled as hard as he could, trying to take the weight off him. Woody hurried back into place and grabbed the stretcher.

"Let's go," Chance called.

Inch by inch the stretcher moved downward. Everyone did their job. No one flinched. No one complained. They just kept holding on with all their strength. The wind blew against them and shook their composure a couple of times, but no one let go. It seemed like hours, but Chance knew it was only minutes before they reached the drilling platform.

For a moment he couldn't move his arm. It was clenched tight, still holding the stretcher. Eventually he yanked it out, as did Kid.

The crew gathered round Cadde, staring at a man Chance was sure they thought invincible. Hell, he did, too. He looked down at his older brother, whose hair was caked with blood, as was the side of his face and his shirt.

There wasn't anything Cadde couldn't do. He'd said High Cotton was going to win the state championship in basketball, even though they were facing a team that hadn't lost all year. With two seconds left in the game, the other team had been ahead by one point. The coach knew that if they could get the ball to

Cadde, he'd make something happen. And he did. He shot a three-pointer from center court at the sound of the buzzer, and High Cotton had its first state championship ever.

As a boy, Cadde would say he was going to own an oil company one day. He'd made that happen, too. Today he was CEO of Shilah Oil.

If he set his mind to it, Cadde could do anything, it seemed, except take a breath. His big body was still inside the straps, and Chance felt a moment of fear.

"Rev up the chopper," he said to Kid. "We have to get him to a hospital."

Kid seemed paralyzed now, unable to move.

"Kid," he shouted, and his brother practically jumped off the platform.

This time Chance grabbed the stretcher with both hands. "I need a little more help, boys, to get him on the chopper."

"Yes, sir." Woody and Mick reached for the stretcher.

"You boys did good today. Real good," Chance told them as they hurried to the aircraft. "We couldn't have saved him without you."

"It's our job, sir." Woody looked embarrassed.

Not quite, Chance thought as they loaded Cadde onto the chopper.

"Mr. Hardin," Sam called above the roar of the helicopter, trying to hold on to his hard hat. "What about the well?"

"Give the boys the rest of the day off. They've earned it. We'll start again in the morning."

As the helicopter lifted off, Chance leaned his back against the wall of the aircraft, the front part of the stretcher resting on his legs. He sucked in much needed air.

"Is he breathing?" Kid asked, navigating the controls.

Chance's eyes were glued to Cadde's chest. There was no movement. He was so afraid. *Don't you die on us, Cadde.* Chance removed his gloves and placed his hand over the leather there. No movement. No breath.

You can do anything. Don't you dare die on us.

Chance curled his other hand into a fist and then brought it down hard atop the one on Cadde's heart. Cadde's chest wall rose and then he coughed. His chest rose again. Cadde was alive and breathing. Chance sank back, exhausted.

"Hot damn," Kid said. "Best sound I ever

heard." He glanced back. "Where are we going?"

"Memorial Hermann. Call and get us a clearance to land on their pad."

"I don't have their number."

"Are you brain-dead?" Chance snapped. "Call Barbara, Cadde's secretary. She'll do it for you."

"It's Sunday, idiot."

"Call her cell. It's an emergency."

The fall had shaken Kid, but the kidder was coming back. On that derrick, though, he'd been dead serious. As serious as Chance had ever seen him, or probably ever would again.

He heard Kid talking to Barbara. "She's calling," he announced. "She'll let us know as soon as she gets us clearance."

"We don't have a lot of time." Chance watched blood ooze through the bandage, and he applied light pressure with his hand.

"I know," Kid said. "If she doesn't call back before we get there, I'm landing anywhere I can."

Chance thought he probably would, and he saw no need to stop him. Cadde needed medical attention fast.

"Prepare for landing," Kid called.

Chance glanced out the window, and all he could see were cars. "Where in the hell...?"

"Welcome to Memorial Hermann parking lot," Kid said, climbing into the back with Chance and Cadde. "Let's get him inside."

"You landed in the parking lot?" Chance was still in shock.

"Hell, yeah." Kid reached for the end of the stretcher, and Chance noticed how blue Kid's right arm was. Chance looked down to see that his was black-and-blue, too.

"Let's go," Kid shouted, and Chance rose to his feet with his hands clamped around the stretcher one more time.

As they were unloading Cadde, two burly guys in white ran toward them. "What the hell do you think you're doing?" one yelled.

"We have an injured man who needs medical attention," Kid yelled back.

"Why didn't you use the helicopter pad?" the other one asked.

"Now that's a long story," Kid told him. "Too long to share here. Could we get a move on, please?"

"What did y'all do to him?" the first guy asked, looking down at Cadde strapped in with ropes and leather.

"That's another long story and—"

The other guy had been on a radio, obviously calling the emergency room. Two more people came running with a stretcher.

"Now we're talking," Kid muttered as they gave up their burden to professionals.

A police siren could be heard in the distance, getting closer and closer.

"You better move that thing." Burly guy number one thumbed toward the chopper. "Evidently the police have been called."

Kid jumped into the helicopter. "I'll be back as soon as I can."

"Call if they arrest you," Chance said.

"Like hell!"

Chance heard the door slam shut. In seconds the helicopter lifted off the pavement, just as two police cars roared onto the scene. Chance ran after the stretcher, choosing to ignore the police—for now. But he knew they would be asking questions.

He filled out paperwork and put Jessie down as next of kin. "I don't have his insurance information," he told the nurse. "It's probably in his wallet. I'll get it to you as soon as I can."

As he walked off, a young woman stepped in front of him. "Mr. Hardin?" Her hand rested on her stomach. She was very pregnant.

"Yes," he answered.

"I'm Brad Coulson's wife, Sherry. Brad's been in surgery a long time, and no one has told us anything. I'm worried." She pointed to two people in their forties sitting in the waiting area. "His parents are worried, too. Could you please get some information for us?"

"I'll do my best," he promised, and went back to the nurse at the desk. Brad was in surgery. That meant he was alive. Thank God!

"Ma'am," he said to the nurse.

She looked up. "Did you forget something, Mr. Hardin?"

"No, actually, an employee of Shilah Oil, Brad Coulson, was brought in a little earlier. His family is here and they'd like to know how he's doing." And so would he.

She typed in something on her keyboard. "Mr. Coulson is still in surgery." She frowned. "What's his family doing in E.R.? They should be in the surgery waiting room."

"No one told us where to go," Sherry said.

Chance turned on all his charm. "Could you please get someone to show them where to go?"

"Yes, of course." She smiled, and he felt a moment of anger. It wasn't Shay's smile.

He had to get her out of his mind.

He left the Coulson family in the hands of the nurse and went to find Cadde. Two double doors greeted him with the message Do Not Enter. Hospital Personnel Only. Without a thought, he pushed through them.

"Hey." A nurse stopped him. "You're not supposed to be in here. You have to go back to the waiting area."

"I'm looking for my brother, Cadde Hardin," he said as if she hadn't spoken.

"The doctor is with him. Now please..."

"Is there a problem?" A man in blue scrubs came out of a room. He scribbled something on a chart and looked up. "Ah, Mr. Hardin. I saw you on the news—very brave rescue."

"News?" Chance hadn't realized he'd spoken aloud until the doctor responded.

"Yes. The rescue is on the news, national even."

Damn! Cadde was going to hate this. This kind of PR they didn't need. He vaguely remembered a man with a camera on his shoulder. At the time they'd been busy trying to save his brother's life and hadn't given it another thought. He should have.

"How's Cadde?"

"He's lost some blood, but not enough for us to give him any. He has a concussion and right now he's undergoing tests, mainly an MRI of his head. I don't want to miss anything. Barring any unforeseen surprises, he should be fine. He's strong and healthy and should recover quickly. We're keeping him overnight for observation. I've already called his wife."

Oh crap! Cadde wasn't going to like this, but Chance would deal with that later.

"Thanks, Doc," he said. "Is he awake?"

"Not yet, but it shouldn't be long." The doctor glanced at his bruised arm. "You should let us look at that."

Chance flexed his fingers. "I'm fine. It's just bruised."

"If you say so." The doctor scribbled something else on the chart. "When your brother finishes the tests, they'll take him up to a room. You can get the number from the nurse at the front desk."

"Thanks, Doc." They shook hands.

"Congratulations on a dangerous but successful rescue," the doctor added. "You get me twelve feet off the ground and I become a wimpy little girl."

"Sometimes you do what you have to."

The doctor nodded and turned away. "Put

some ice on that arm," he called over his shoulder.

Chance flexed his arm and pain shot up his shoulder into his back. A reminder of the day.

He got the room number from the nurse and went upstairs. Sinking into a chair outside the door, he waited for Cadde. Nurses and other staff milled around him. People were coming and going. But he'd never felt more alone in his life.

Green eyes flashed through his mind. God, he needed her to hold him. He needed her to be here. But Shay was never going to be in his life again.

Not ever.

Chapter Fourteen

Shay went through the motions of the day for Darcy. Beth had wanted her daughter to have a foundation of faith, so Shay did her best to get her to church on Sundays. Darcy loved her Bible study class and was making new friends. Separating her and Petey for a while had been a good idea. It had given her daughter the incentive—and courage—to reach out when otherwise she wouldn't have.

A lot of that had to do with Chance. He lifted Darcy's low self-esteem just by being in her life and with words of encouragement. He taught her that fighting wasn't the answer and that a smile and friendship went a long way.

How did Shay tell Darcy that Chance, who she considered a giant among men, wasn't coming back? And it was all Shay's fault.

If she had told Chance the truth from the start, all this pain could have been avoided. But then she would never have known what a wonderful man he was. She would never have fallen in love and experienced those all-consuming, mind-blowing passionate feelings. Never again would those emotions consume her—because she would never love anyone like she loved Chance.

The pain of hurting him was too raw for her to think much further.

The Home Health attendant was with Blanche, and Shay went to let her know she had returned. The woman left. Blanche had had a bath and looked refreshed—almost happy, staring at those damn rings.

"Do you need anything?"

"No," Blanche replied, twisting her hand. "I have everything I need."

Shay sighed and walked across the hall to her room to change. She slipped into denim shorts and paused. Chance had said he liked her in shorts. The warm memory floated away as she recalled what had happened next.

Grabbing a sleeveless knit top, she yanked it over her head and went to find her daughter.

Darcy was sitting on the floor going through her workbook from Bible study.

"What do you want for lunch, sweetie?"

"Hot dogs," Darcy shouted.

Hot dogs. Oh, God, was everything going to remind Shay of Chance?

"Think healthy," she said. "How about left-over roast?"

Darcy frowned. "No. We had that yesterday." Her eyes suddenly brightened. "Fish sticks and mac and cheese."

"Darcy."

"Mom."

They had a standoff and Shay was the first to give in. "Oh, okay. Now go change your clothes."

Darcy skipped to her room.

Shay set about preparing lunch. While the macaroni boiled, she made Blanche a protein smoothie and carried it to her. She hurried back to the kitchen, followed by Darcy.

"Is it ready, Mom?" she asked.

"Not yet."

"I'm gonna watch cartoons then."

"Okay."

Shay was setting the food on the table when Darcy screamed, "Chance!"

Shay dropped a hot pad and ran into the living room to look outside. Had Chance come back?

"Not there. Here." Darcy pointed to the TV.

Shay walked slowly to stand in front of the screen. Breaking News—Live Coverage flashed across the screen. The shot panned to a large oil rig, the derrick reaching toward the sky. Men on one side of the structure looked toward another one hanging upside down in thin air. No. No! That couldn't be Chance.

The camera then zoomed in on a man at the top of the derrick. "We're told this is Chance Hardin, and his brother Cisco is below," the reporter was saying. "The man hanging is Cadde Hardin, their brother and CEO of Shilah Oil. Our source tells us that Mr. Hardin slipped after rescuing a roughneck who may have had a heart attack. That man has been taken to Memorial Hermann. There's no word on his condition yet. If you look closely you'll see a single rope is holding Mr. Hardin up there as his brothers try to save his life. This is dangerous, very dangerous, so if you have a weak stomach I suggest you not watch."

Shay backed toward the kitchen and grabbed her purse. One thing kept running through her mind—that Chance was going to die believing she didn't love him. No. She couldn't let that happen. Suddenly it seemed so simple. Tell him the whole truth and let the broken pieces of their hearts fall where they may. Living a lie wasn't acceptable anymore.

"Darcy, sweetie. I want you to do something for me." Shay clicked off the TV. She didn't want Darcy watching it.

"Aw, Mom," Darcy complained.

"I have to go and check on Chance. I need you to stay here and help Blanche."

"What?"

Shay had never asked this of her before, so Darcy was naturally confused. Nettie was at a flea market and wouldn't be home until one. That was too long to wait.

"If Blanche calls for me, go see what she wants. If she wants water, get her a glass. She likes to suck on hard candy so if she asks for it, please get it. Tell her I'll be back as soon as I can. If she's rude to you, just walk out of the room. Understand?"

"Yes, Mommy, I can do it."

Shay kissed her forehead. "I'm proud of you. Your lunch is on the table. Do not turn on the stove and do not go outside. Nettie will be here shortly."

"I got it." Darcy nodded and went into the kitchen to eat.

Shay put on a movie for her to watch and then removed the batteries from the remote control. She didn't want her watching the rescue in case something went wrong. And then she was on her way to find Chance.

A loud stomping sound jerked Chance out of his somber thoughts. He looked up to see Kid running his way, his work boots pounding on the tiled floor. Chance jumped to his feet.

"Are the cops after you?"

"Hell, no." Kid sank down beside him.

"You do know they will be. They couldn't miss Shilah Oil written across that chopper."

"I'll handle it then. How's Cadde? Is he going to make it?"

Now Chance knew what the rush was all about. Serious Kid was back. "Relax," he said. "Cadde has a concussion and some bruises, but the doctor said he'll be fine. He's undergoing tests right now to make sure they didn't miss anything."

"Thank God." Kid sagged in the chair as

if someone had let all the air out of him. "He looked like hell. I thought…"

"Cadde's going to be fine," Chance assured him.

Kid sat up straight, staring at Chance's arm. "Damn. Those are some bad bruises." He held out his own arm. "Mine's not that bad."

"I was trying to keep the weight off you and to keep us from tumbling down."

There was silence for a while. They both knew they would have suffered a lot more to save their brother's life.

Then Kid slapped him on the back. "Dad said we were tough. I guess he was right."

"Yeah," Chance murmured, and he felt no bitterness at the mention of their father. He had finally put it behind him. The ache in his chest was about something entirely different. It was about a green-eyed lady who had broken his heart.

Down the hall, elevator doors opened and two nurses pushed a gurney toward them, with a doctor following. They got to their feet when they saw the patient was Cadde. He was still pale and out for the count.

They shook hands with the doctor. "How is he?" Chance asked.

"Fine. The MRI didn't show anything, so in a few days Mr. Hardin should be back to normal—a little sore, with a bruised head, but normal. We're keeping him overnight for observation. He can go home in the morning."

"Thanks, Doc," Kid said.

"No problem." The doctor walked away, but turned back. "Whoever strapped him into that contraption strapped him in to stay. There are welts across his chest and legs from the tight leather. He's probably going to be pissed about that, but I figure you guys can handle him."

"You bet." Kid grinned. "We've handled Cadde pissed more times than we can count."

The doctor strolled away, smiling.

Chance and Kid walked into the room. One of the nurses was checking his IV, then straightened the sheet over Cadde. "He should wake up soon," she said.

"Thank you, ma'am," Kid replied, eyeing her from head to toe.

Chance poked him in the ribs. "Focus," he whispered under his breath.

With a slight smile the nurse walked out of the room.

"Give it a rest, Kid," Chance said, making his way to the bed.

Kid stood on the other side. "When do you think he'll wake up?"

"When he's ready, I guess."

Almost on cue, Cadde's eyelashes fluttered and his eyes opened slowly. "Where am I?" he groaned.

"In a hospital," Kid answered.

"What…what happened?"

"You don't remember?" Chance asked.

"Brad was hurt and I—"

"Yeah. You slipped off the derrick," Kid interrupted. "There were ten or more rough-necks ready to climb up there to rescue Brad, but oh no, you had to do it. You had to show them you're the big boss and still have what it takes." It seemed as if someone had waved a green flag in front of Kid and he couldn't stop. "You're facing forty, and sit all day and half the night at a desk. What were you thinking? I've traipsed all over Texas chasing your damn dream and you pull something like this. I…" Suddenly Kid ran out of fuel.

"Did you get it off your chest?" Cadde asked.

"Hell, no," he shouted. "When you get out of here I'm going to kill you." He flopped into a chair and rested his dirty boots on the bed. "You know that song that says 'He ain't heavy, he's my brother'? Well, let me tell you, brother, you're heavy as hell. Take a look at Chance's arm."

Cadde turned his head and stared. "What happened?"

Before Chance could answer, Kid grabbed the remote control and turned on the TV. "You want to know what happened? Take a look. They're running it about every fifteen minutes. Must be a slow news day."

"Kid." Chance tried to stop him, but it was too late. The rescue blasted onto the screen.

Cadde watched in silence for a few minutes and then said, "Turn it off."

Chance yanked the control from Kid and did so.

"Has Jessie seen it?" he asked.

"She'd have to live in a cave not to," Kid muttered.

Cadde turned to Chance. "Make sure the hospital doesn't call her."

"They already have."

"What?"

"She's your wife, remember?" Kid reminded him. "Next of kin sort of thing."

"Shit." Cadde moved restlessly in the bed, then winced.

Kid got to his feet. "On that note I'm going

to my apartment to crash. Hopefully I can persuade that pretty nurse to go with me. I bet she could ease my aches and pains."

Chance just shook his head.

"I'm glad you're gonna make it, big brother," Kid told him, "but the next time I have to risk my life to save yours I'm—"

"Have you forgotten all the times I've risked mine to save yours? Remember that woman in Laredo? She forgot to tell you she was married, or you chose to ignore it. But you were very aware of it when her husband held a shotgun to your head. Who kept him from spreading your brains across that barroom? And what about those two girls in Lubbock who found out you were dating them at the same time? Who took the knife away and kept those she-devils from spreading your balls across Texas?"

Kid shuffled his feet. "So I guess we're even."

"Until the next crisis," Chance interjected.

"Until the next crisis." Kid stretched out his hand to Cadde and he took it. They held on longer than necessary. Chance knew Kid wasn't really angry about what he'd had to do. He was angry he could have lost his sidekick, his brother, today.

Cadde turned to Chance. "How's Brad?"

"He's still in surgery. I'll check on him a little later."

"Good." Cadde nodded and winced again. Chance knew he probably had a gigantic headache. "Have you got the rig started again?"

"No."

"Why not?" he demanded.

"I'm easing my weary bones out the door," Kid said. "I don't have any fight left, so Chance, he's all yours."

"Why not?" Cadde demanded again as soon as Kid had left.

"Because those guys went through a harrowing experience today and they need a break. We'll start again in the morning."

"Like hell. You'll start now."

Chance was tired and his body ached. Any patience he'd possessed had completely flown the coop. He walked to the edge of the bed and stared his brother in the eye. "The rig starts in the morning," he stated in a firm tone. "A lot of roughnecks worked together to save your hide today. To me that deserves recognition, so I gave them time off with pay. If you override my order, I'm outta here for good. What's it going to be?"

Cadde moved restlessly and Chance saw him wince again. Clearly he was in pain, but he'd never admit it. Big, stubborn oaf!

"Okay." Cadde sighed. "But it better start in the morning."

Chance swung toward the door. "Get some rest—I definitely need some. See you tomorrow."

"Chance," Cadde called.

He looked back at his brother.

"Thanks."

Chance nodded and walked out. Outside the door, he took a long breath. Down the hall he could see Kid talking to the nurse. Dealing with his brothers was like dealing with two petulant children. What had he gotten himself into?

A tap-tapping sound caught his attention. He looked up to see Jessie Murdock Hardin coming toward him. She wore a burgundy print dress with a short black jacket. Her dark brown hair was coiled at her neck. Sunglasses perched on the top of her head. She was beautiful, sophisticated and a woman to be reckoned with. It showed in every line of her slim body. Why she and Cadde couldn't make the marriage work was beyond him.

"How's Cadde?" she asked, stopping by his side.

"He's going to be fine."

"Good. I didn't think anything could penetrate that thick skull of his." She moved to the door. "I got the paperwork on the transfer of shares into your name. Of course, Cadde told me nothing about it. The papers just arrived on my desk. I started not to sign off on them, but that would have been spiteful. You'll be a great asset to Shilah Oil and I was happy to sign, despite Cadde's lack of business manners."

"Thank you, Jessie," Chance said as she went into the room.

Cadde hadn't told her. That boggled Chance's mind. He'd sunk everything he had into Cadde's oil venture and his brother hadn't told Jessie, the woman who held all the power at Shilah Oil. Damn! He and Cadde had to have a long talk.

Kid strolled toward him. "Hey, the nurse, Molly, has a friend. Want to go out tonight?"

"Are you out of your mind? I'm going to the apartment to rest—alone."

"Okay. Don't blow a gasket." Kid gestured toward Cadde's door. "What did Jessie want?"

"To see her husband."

"Really? I thought she'd phone in her get well wishes."

"That's cold, Kid, even for you."

"She keeps him on tenterhooks all the time."

"Maybe he keeps *her* on tenterhooks," Chance retorted. "I don't know and I'm not getting involved in their marriage."

"Whoa." Kid held up his hands. "I think Chance needs a nap."

"Go away, Kid."

"I'm going." He headed back to the nurse's station. "Sure you won't change your mind?" he called over his shoulder.

Chance didn't answer. He didn't feel he needed to. He ran his hands over his face. What a horrible day. Once again he stood alone in the hallway, feeling lonelier than ever. His arms ached for Shay and he couldn't shake that feeling. He wondered how long it took to get over a broken heart.

He glanced down the hallway and blinked. Was that...? The woman looked like Shay, with all that blonde hair cascading down her back. She spoke to a nurse. Was he so tired he was imagining her? The nurse pointed to him, and Shay took off at a run.

Was he dreaming?

Chapter Fifteen

As Shay reached him he did the only thing he could: held out his arms. She barreled into him, almost knocking him off his feet. He held her even though he knew he shouldn't.

"I'm sorry. I was scared, but I love you. Just know that I love you." Her arms clasped him tightly around the neck, her breath fanning the side of his face.

He breathed in the lavender scent of her hair and rejoiced in the feel of her against him. But it couldn't be this easy. He had to have answers.

"How's your brother?" she asked.

"He's going to be fine."

"Good."

"Shay." He eased away from her. "Yesterday you didn't love me. Today you do. To say the least, I'm a little confused."

"I'm sorry." She stroked his face. "I can explain, but it's a long story. I can't do it here. Darcy is with Blanche and I have to run. I'll be at your apartment about six. Okay?"

"Okay." He gathered her into his arms once more and felt her heart beating against his. She loved him. He wasn't going to look that gift horse in the mouth. Besides, he didn't have the energy to keep resisting something he wanted so badly.

He kissed her with all the longing inside him and then just held her as the loneliness ebbed away. In her arms he felt as if he'd found home, a place of peace and trust that only she could create.

After a brief kiss she pulled away. "See you tonight." And she disappeared as quickly as she had arrived.

Just know that I love you.

Like a starving man, he could live on that—for a very long time.

Shay rushed through the back door feeling as if she'd been granted a reprieve—for now. Tonight she had to tell him the truth, and then… She didn't want to think beyond that.

Placing her purse on the kitchen table, she noted the house was very quiet, except for the movie running on the TV. Where was Darcy? Her heart jumped into her throat.

"Darcy!" she shouted.

"Mom's home," she heard her say, and in a second Darcy raced into the room, Tiny, as always, behind her. "Did you see Chance?"

"Yes, sweetie, and he's fine."

"Is he coming here?"

"No. He has to rest, but I'm going to check on him later."

"Can I go, too?"

Shay hated to douse that hope in her daughter's eyes, but tonight was for her and Chance alone. "No, sweetie."

"Shoot." Darcy snapped her fingers.

"Did Nettie come over?"

"Yes, and I told her I had everything under control, so she went home to take a nap."

Shay knew they depended on her too much, but Nettie was all she had. Shay was there for Nettie, too, so she supposed it worked both ways. And that's what families did—depended on each other.

She nodded toward the hallway. "What were you doing?"

"Playing checkers with Blanche," Darcy said, as if it was something she did every day.

"What?"

"Yeah. She beat me, too."

"What brought that on?" Shay was more than curious. Blanche never made any effort to get to know Darcy. She just wanted her out of the house.

Her daughter shrugged. "She asked for some water and I got it with ice and a napkin, just like you do. Then she wanted to know what I was doing and I said nothing 'cause the TV is broke. I couldn't get it off the movie, Mom. It's broken."

"I'll take a look at it," she offered with a sly grin.

"Blanche said it's not much fun when you have nothing to do. I told her that if Petey was here we could play checkers, and that I always beat him. She asked if I could beat her. I said I didn't know. She said get the checkers, and I did. We've been playing...oh, I gotta go back. We have to finish a game."

Darcy darted off and Shay leaned against the counter, thinking, *"Yes, Virginia, there is a Santa Claus."*

Now she just needed to keep the miracles coming.

* * *

Chance woke up stretched across his bed in Jockey shorts. The ice that was supposed to be on his arm was now against his waist. Damn! He sat up and glanced at his watch. Six o'clock and Shay wasn't here. He'd give her time. She could be caught in traffic.

Grabbing a robe, he headed for the kitchen and fresh ice. He sat on the sofa and positioned his arm on a pillow so the pack wouldn't fall off, then he leaned his head back and waited for Shay. At six-thirty he was still waiting.

Had she lied? He had to get off the Shay merry-go-round. It was about to kill him.

He got up and went into the kitchen, and was reaching into the freezer for more ice when his cell buzzed. He looked around. Where was it? He made a mad dash to the bedroom and clicked on.

"Chance, I can't get in. The door is locked." Her voice had never sounded more wonderful.

"I'll be right there." He tied the belt on his robe and slipped on flip-flops. No one was in the building, so he didn't have to worry about his wardrobe. It seemed to take forever for the elevator to get to the bottom level. He quickly opened the outer door and yanked Shay inside, pulling her into his arms.

"I thought you weren't coming," he muttered against the side of her face, the feel of her skin igniting every emotion in him.

"Darcy wanted to come and it took a while to make her understand that she couldn't."

He swept Shay onto the elevator and into his arms again, kissing her long and deep. He didn't have any plans of letting her go anytime soon. They sidestepped from the elevator, across the hall and into the apartment without their lips losing contact. Chance kicked the door shut.

"Chance, wait…" Shay pulled away.

"I don't want to wait," he murmured, trying to capture her lips again. But she held her head back.

"Where's your phone?"

He pointed to an end table. She picked up his cell, poked in a number and handed the device to him. "Tell Darcy you're okay and you'll see her whenever."

"Hey, hotshot," he said when Darcy answered.

"Chance, are you okay?"

"I'm fine now that your mom is here." He kissed Shay lightly.

"I said a prayer for you."

"I appreciate that, hotshot. Thank you. It must have worked 'cause I feel much better."

"I'll say another."

"Thank you, and be good for Nettie."

"I will. Bye."

He laid the phone down and reached for Shay, molding her body against his. She moaned.

"*Chance*... We need to talk."

He shook his head. "No waiting. No talking. Just you and me, right here, right now."

"But..." His tongue licked the corner of her mouth in a provocative gesture. What was left of her control snapped.

"No buts, either." He groaned. "I want you to ease every ache in me, every ache. And so we're clear, it's not just sex."

"No." She bit his earlobe. "It's not just sex. It's a lot more."

"Yes." He took her hand and led her to the bedroom. Sitting on the bed, he pulled her between his legs and started undoing the buttons on her blouse.

As he unfastened her bra, she pushed the robe from his shoulders and gasped.

"What?"

"You're hurt," she said, gazing at his black-and-blue arm. "Oh, Chance, you're so bruised."

"It'll heal."

"You should put some ice on it or something."

"It can wait. Everything can wait." He teased one nipple. "But this."

"Oh, Chance."

He lay back on the bed and pulled her on top of him. Nothing was said for some time, but their moans and sighs filled the room.

When Chance woke up it was six o'clock in the morning. He reached for Shay, but knew she wasn't there. He sat up and noticed the note on the nightstand.

Sorry I had to leave. You were sleeping so peacefully I couldn't wake you. Talk to you tonight. Love you, Shay.

"Love you" stayed with him while he dressed, and he had a feeling it was going to stay with him the rest of the day. He called Sam from his office to see if the rig was running, pulling pipe to get to the broken one. It was. He said he was on his way, to make sure the rig was drilling by nightfall.

As he headed out, he paused by the elevator for a moment, his thoughts on his older brother. On impulse he walked to Cadde's office. He was shocked to see Barbara at her desk. She usually didn't come in this early.

"Good morning, Mr. Hardin. Can I help you?"

"Nah. I'm fine."

He moved toward Cadde's door and Barbara jumped to her feet. "Mr. Hardin…"

"You don't want me to go in there, do you?"

"I'd rather that you didn't," she replied.

"And I'd rather that I did." Without another word, he stepped inside. And there was Cadde, sitting in his big chair, staring out at the view of Houston with a bandage on his head.

"Have you lost your mind?" he berated Cadde, for what it was worth.

"I couldn't take one more minute in that hospital."

"Did you call Jessie?"

"No."

"How can you be so inconsiderate?" Chance reached for his phone. Jessie informed him that she already knew because the hospital had notified her.

As Chance shoved his phone into its leather cover, he heard loud voices in Barbara's office. Obviously, Kid was trying to get past the watchdog. In a moment he burst through the door.

"Ah, Chance, I was over at the hospital and…" His eyes swung to Cadde. "Son of a bitch!"

"You two can go to work now," Cadde said in a flat tone.

"How did you get here?" Kid demanded.

"I called Barbara and she brought my clothes this morning. I always keep some here in the office."

"There's a lot in the apartment, too," Chance added. "Do you even know where home is?"

"As I said, you two can—"

"Like hell." Kid stomped farther into the room. "You're not working today, period."

Cadde ignored him and turned to Chance. "Are they pulling pipe on Crocker Number One?"

"Yep. I'm on my way there now."

"Forget about the damn well for one day," Kid yelled, moving toward Cadde. He motioned to Chance, who stepped to Cadde's right.

"Now we can do this the easy way or the hard way. You can march yourself down the hall to the apartment and go to bed or we're going to throw your ass out this window. Which do you think would be less painful?"

"Kid, you'd better—"

Before Cadde could finish what he had to say, Kid and Chance each grabbed an arm of the chair and rolled Cadde out of his office and through Barbara's, whose eyes opened wide in shock. Down the hall to the apartment they went. Cadde tried to stop the chair with his feet, but soon found that was dangerous. In the apartment they maneuvered him into the master bedroom and uploaded him onto the bed.

Cadde stretched out. "I'm so damn tired."

Kid looked at Chance. "Should we tie him to the headboard?"

They heard a snore and saw that Cadde was asleep.

"Guess not," Chance answered. "He seems worn-out."

"Yeah." Kid pushed the chair back down the hall. "I'll check on him later."

"And I'm off to the Crocker well."

Chance spent the morning with the roughnecks as they continued to pull up pipe, trying to reach the broken one. He didn't offer any assistance because he knew they were well equipped to do it.

As soon as he got off the chopper, the crew had started firing questions at him. "How's Mr. Hardin? How's Brad?" Chance was happy to tell them that everyone was fine. He'd checked on Brad before leaving the hospital the night before. The by-pass surgery was a success, and Brad was resting comfortably in CCU with his wife by his side.

Chance had had a chance to speak with the doctor, who said Brad had to change his diet, his lifestyle, and get more exercise. Roughnecking was one of things that had to go. Brad was grounded for life, but Chance was sure he was glad to be alive to witness the birth of his first child.

At noon they reached the broken pipe and had it out of the hole in record time. "Good job," Chance shouted above the roar of the rig. "Let's start reconnecting pipe and get back to drilling."

"Yes, sir," Woody said.

Chance climbed down the ladder and removed his gloves.

Sam walked up to him. "They work harder when you're here."

He nodded. "That's the reason for the visit. I want this rig drilling again."

"I'll let you know when it happens."

"Thanks, Sam. I'm going back to Shilah Oil. If anything comes up, call me."

"Will do. Have a safe trip."

Chance was back at the apartment by two. He peeped into Cadde's room, and found him still sound asleep. And Kid hadn't had to tie him to the bed.

After showering, Chance changed into clean clothes and then headed to the kitchen for ice, because his arm was throbbing. He paused in the doorway. Cadde was sitting on the sofa.

"Hey, you're up."

"Yeah. They reach the broken pipe?"

Chance sighed. It was always the oil business for Cadde. Nothing else mattered.

"Yes. Sam's going to call when they start drilling."

"Good. And Brad? How's he doing?"

"Resting comfortably."

"Good." Cadde laid his head against the leather. "I feel as if some fat lady is tap-dancing on my head."

"It's probably just Kid."

"Nah, he's the pain in my ass." Cadde turned his head to look at Chance. "Do you have anything to eat in this place?"

"Not much. I'll go get us something," he

offered, forgetting about his arm. "I haven't eaten, either."

In thirty minutes he was back with chicken fried steaks, baked potatoes, the works. They sat at the table to eat and Chance's thoughts, as they often did, shifted to Shay.

"You're not staying here tonight, are you?"

"Don't worry, little brother," Cadde said around a mouthful of steak. "I'm going home to get a lecture from Jessie, I'm sure."

"She has a right to be angry." Chance thought of what Jessie had said to him last night. "Why didn't you tell her you were bringing me into the business? I sank my life savings into this venture and she might not have signed off on it."

"I sent her the papers. There was nothing to discuss. Your shares come out of my twenty-five percent. I don't see a problem."

Chance watched his brother. "You're not that inconsiderate."

He took a swallow of his iced tea. "Okay. I'm having a hard time with Jessie. When Roscoe made his wishes known, she didn't object or get angry. She accepted the marriage. But now it's very clear she's upset."

"Well, big brother, you need to talk to your wife."

"Yeah." Cadde twisted his plastic cup. "If she hadn't signed off on the deal, I would have done something."

"Mmm." Marriage wasn't supposed to be a business arrangement. Cadde was going to have to bend, and Chance knew that would be hard for him.

"When are you going to find a place?"

Chance leaned back and stretched his sore arm. "A Realtor sent over some listings, but I haven't had time to look at them." His whole world had fallen apart and he couldn't have cared less. But now...

They carried their iced tea into the living room. "Is it serious with Shay?" Cadde asked, easing onto the sofa.

"Very," he replied, unable to keep the grin from his face.

"That was fast. You've only known her—"

Kid burst through the door, interrupting them.

"Haven't got that knocking thing down, have you?" Chance asked.

"Don't start with the manners lecture," he told him, and stepped over Cadde's long legs to sit on the sofa.

"There are bruises on my chest and legs," Cadde commented. "The doctor said it was from the straps of the medical cage, that I'm guessing was tightened by the two of you."

Kid bumped Cadde's shoulder with his fist. "Yep. We made sure you weren't coming out of that thing. You can thank us any time."

"Have you seen these bruises?"

The phone connected to Cadde's office rang, preventing him from displaying his boo-boos. Chance hit the speaker button. "What is it, Barbara?"

"There are two policemen here. They want to see the CEO of Shilah Oil."

"What do they want?" Cadde asked.

"They didn't say."

"I'll be right there." Cadde stood and stared at Kid. "What have you done?"

Kid looked at Chance, who stared back. Confession time.

Kid ran his hands down the thighs of his jeans. "Now, Cadde, you're going to laugh at this."

"I'm not laughing now."

"Okay." He shrugged. "I landed the chopper in the hospital parking lot."

"What?"

"You were bleeding to death and we couldn't get clearance for the pad in time, so I landed it where I could. I'd do it again to save your sorry ass."

Chance could see the laughter bubbling up in Cadde's eyes. "You landed the chopper in a parking lot? A chopper that has Shilah Oil written on it bigger than Dallas?"

"Yep," Kid answered.

Cadde burst out laughing, which was very rare. He was always so focused, so serious.

Sobering quickly, he added, "Well, boys, let's go talk to the cops, and for Kid's sake, I hope they're both women."

Chapter Sixteen

Only one of the officers was a woman. She stood six feet tall and looked as though she could bench-press Kid without a problem.

Cadde took a seat, but the officers in blue, Chance and Kid all remained standing.

"Mr. Hardin," the male officer said to Cadde. "The E.R. people confirmed yesterday that you'd been injured. We went back to the hospital this morning to speak with you, but you had gone."

"I was released."

"The hospital doesn't have a record of that."

"Well, let's just say I left voluntarily."

The officer pulled a small notebook from

his shirt pocket. "We have a report of a Shilah Oil helicopter landing in Memorial Hermann's parking lot early yesterday afternoon."

"I was piloting the aircraft." Kid spoke up. "My brother was bleeding to death and I had to get him to a doctor. Since we couldn't get clearance for the pad, I landed wherever I could."

"That was very dangerous, Mr. Hardin."

"I made sure no one was in the way and that I had room to land the craft."

"It's illegal to land in a business area parking lot," the female officer told him.

"Ah, ma'am." Kid walked closer to her and Chance groaned inwardly. "My brother was hurt and I didn't know what else to do."

He gazed into her eyes like a puppy waiting for a bone. How did Kid do that so easily?

"That's understandable," the woman replied, her eyes never leaving his.

"It's illegal," the male officer reminded her.

"You know what's illegal?" Kid's tone was sharp, and Chance knew a whole lot of attitude was about to fly out of his mouth.

Chance grabbed a fistful of his brother's shirt from the back and squeezed, reminding him who he was talking to.

"It's that killer smile of yours." Kid switched gears and turned back to the woman, his charm on full blast. She seemed to wither.

"Stick to business, Mr. Hardin," the male officer snapped, shoving the notebook back into his pocket. "Under the circumstances I'm not going to cite you for an unauthorized landing. Next time use the pad."

Chance had the feeling Kid was going to salute, but he couldn't, because Chance still held his shirt tight.

The two officers walked to the door. The woman smiled back at Kid.

"Now that would be an unauthorized landing," Kid remarked when the door closed. "And let go of my damn shirt."

All three brothers burst out laughing.

"I'm waiting for the day when you grow up," Cadde said. "I've given up hope that it will be anytime soon."

"He was all grown up on that derrick," Chance said. "If you'll look closely at the video, you might see a tear or two in his eyes."

"There was not," Kid exclaimed, flopping into a chair and resting his boots on Cadde's desk.

There was silence for a moment, and then

Cadde said, "I appreciate what both of you did. Thank you."

Kid rubbed his eyes in jest. "Now I am going to tear up."

"That's a no-no," Cadde reminded him. "Dad said men don't cry."

"Yeah." Chance rubbed his hands together. "Another one of his senseless beliefs."

"Let's don't talk about Dad," Kid pleaded. "I get flashes of white anger when we do."

"Let it go, Kid," Chance said. "I have."

"Have you, really?" He lifted an eyebrow in disbelief.

"I'm not living with that bitterness anymore."

"We still don't know who the woman was," Cadde mused.

"What difference would it make?" Chance asked. A day didn't go by that he didn't think about the woman who'd torn his parents apart. He was getting better at pushing those thoughts away, though. He was happy with Shay and he didn't want the past to invade their relationship.

Cadde's phone buzzed and Barbara's voice came on. "Mr. Hardin, Thaddeus Jones is here to see you."

"Send him in," Cadde said.

Kid jumped up and opened the door. "Thaddeus T-Bone Jones, where in the hell have you been keeping yourself?"

T-Bone was an old friend of their father's. They'd both started working in the oil fields when they were eighteen, and had become friends, best friends. T-Bone had eaten at their dinner table many a night. The man was now a little older, a lot grayer, and a sight for sore eyes in worn jeans, a Western shirt and boots. He leaned heavily on a cane.

"Mostly at home in Giddings," T-Bone answered. "I'm getting too old to traipse around those oil fields making money for the big man." He glanced about. "Ain't this something? I'm impressed. Ol' Chuck would be proud. His boys are in the oil business." He paused. "I saw Cadde dangling like hang down sausage on the TV, and I had to come and see for myself, since I was in Houston for a checkup. Had knee surgery a few months back."

"How are you doing?" Chance shook his hand. "Have a seat."

T-Bone squinted at him. "Is that you, Chance? My God, you've grown into a tall sucker. You were knee high to a grasshopper when I last saw you."

"That was when you came to visit us at Aunt Etta's after the funeral."

"Yep." T-Bone eased into a chair, placing the cane beside him. "Sad, sad day when we lost ol' Chuck."

"We lost our mom, too," Chance reminded him.

"Yep. Didn't make 'em better than Carol." T-Bone glanced at Cadde and Cadde stood to shake the man's hand. "So you're the big man now? You're filling Roscoe's shoes?"

"I'm giving it a whirl."

"Chuck always said that you would make it one day, and Kid and Chance would follow you. Guess he was right."

"Yeah," Kid said with a smirk. "We follow him around like two little puppies."

"Still quick-witted." T-Bone laughed.

"Dim-witted is more like it," Cadde said under his breath, and sat on the edge of his desk facing T-Bone. "We were just talking about Dad."

Chance knew exactly where Cadde was going. T-Bone had known their father better than anyone, and if he'd had a mistress T-Bone would know. Why hadn't Chance thought of it before? T-Bone could have the answers to all his tormented questions.

His stomach roiled with uneasiness. It was as if he didn't want to know the truth anymore, which was ridiculous. It would give them some sort of peace.

"Fine man," T-Bone muttered.

"Does a fine man cheat on his wife?" Cadde asked.

T-Bone drew back, affronted. "Why would you ask something like that?"

"Because Dad was cheating on Mom," Chance told him, unable to hold the words in. "You see, T-Bone, I was sleeping in the backseat of the car that night, but Mom and Dad screaming at each other woke me up. He said he was in love with someone else and he was leaving High Cotton and his family behind." Chance took a breath. "Who was the woman?"

"Now, Chance, your father was a good man."

"Who was she?" Chance shouted. "How did he meet her?"

T-Bone fiddled with his cane and then said in a low tone, "He met her in Giddings."

"She was from around High Cotton?" Kid asked.

"No." The older man shook his head. "She was from Houston, but she was working in the diner for some reason. I don't know why." He heaved a sigh and clasped his hands on the cane. "Chuck and I stopped in there for lunch one day. Your mom was busy doing something at the school for you boys. When the waitress heard Chuck was from High Cotton, she latched on to him, pressing up against him, asking questions. She was a pretty thing, blonde and curvy. I told Chuck he'd better be careful, and he said it didn't hurt to look."

"But it turned into something more?" Chance asked in a voice he didn't recognize.

"Yeah. She wouldn't leave him alone. She kept calling, and I know Carol was getting suspicious."

That's why his mom had talked to Renee. She knew her husband was cheating, but she didn't want to face it. Son of a bitch! Anger coiled through him.

"Who was she?" he shouted again.

"Now, Chance, you're getting angry for no reason. The past is done. Let it go."

"Who was she?" he asked in a calmer voice.

T-Bone studied his cane for a moment. "Jack's ex."

Chance suddenly lost his voice. He couldn't mean…

"Jack who?" Kid asked the question Chance couldn't articulate.

"Jack Calhoun's ex, Blanche Dumont."

If the floor had opened up and swallowed him, Chance wouldn't have been more shocked. *Blanche Dumont. Shay's mother.* It couldn't be.

Cadde watched him for a second, then turned back to T-Bone. "She was older than Dad."

"By a few years," T-Bone answered. "But she was still a looker."

"What happened next?" Kid asked. "Did she have an apartment or something where he visited her?"

"In the beginning, I guess, but I went into the diner one day to see if I could talk her into leaving him alone. Ed said she didn't work there anymore. Evidently Jack had sent her a message through his foreman, Harland. She could leave Giddings of her own free will or she could leave in a coffin. It was her choice. Ed said she left on a bus that afternoon."

"Did Dad follow her?" Cadde asked.

"Oh, yeah, she made sure he did. She called and told him where she lived. Every chance he got he was at her house. He spent long weekends with her, telling Carol he was working overtime."

"Why didn't you stop him?" Chance yelled. "You were his best friend. He listened to you."

"Don't you think I tried?" T-Bone raised his voice for the first time. "She had her hooks into him and nothing I said mattered. He just wanted her." T-Bone pushed himself to his feet. "I'm sorry, boys. I really am."

"We know," Cadde assured him. "It's just a little hard for us to understand."

"When Chuck met her, he changed into someone I didn't know. He wasn't the same ol' fun-loving guy." T-Bone shuffled to the door. "I'm real proud of you boys, and as I said, Chuck would be, too. Try to remember the dad you loved. The man who wrestled with you in the backyard, taught you how to throw a ball and helped you with your FFA projects. I mean, you don't take a steer to the Houston Fat Stock Show and win grand prize without someone teaching you something along the way."

"Somehow those moments don't mean a thing when your dad runs out on you." Kid spoke the words that were in Chance's heart. "It tarnishes them in a way I can't explain."

T-Bone nodded in understanding. "Try to

find some peace, boys, because you can't go forward if you keep looking back. Good luck in the oil business."

They shook hands and T-Bone left.

The three of them stood lost in their thoughts.

Chance shoved his hands into his jeans pockets, looking out at the busy metropolis of Houston. Blanche, Shay's mother, was his father's lover. He had a hard time grasping that.

"Chance."

He turned to Cadde.

"Did you ever see Blanche when you were visiting Shay?"

"No. She's bedridden. I asked once to meet her, but Shay said she didn't like people seeing her in her condition."

"Or she was keeping you two apart," Kid suggested.

"Shay doesn't know," he said. "If she did, she would have told me. She wouldn't keep something like that from me."

"Are you sure?" Kid pressed.

"Shut up, Kid."

"You're not sure. That's why you're angry."

"Kid…"

Cadde got between them. "Leave Chance

alone. He has to sort this out on his own and deal with it."

"And I will." He headed for the door and didn't look back. He had to see Shay and couldn't wait until six.

For years, not knowing the truth had tortured him. Now that he knew who the woman was, he was still tortured. Nothing seemed to ease the pain of that awful night. Would it haunt him for the rest of his life? Shay was the only one who could ease the turmoil inside him.

He parked at Shay's house behind a white Honda Civic. Obviously, she had company. As he made his way to the door, it opened and a woman came out.

"Good afternoon," she said pleasantly.

He tipped his hat. "Good afternoon."

"I'm the Home Health attendant and I was just leaving. Are you here to see Blanche?"

"Yes," he replied. It was time he met the lady. He walked inside and closed the door. Shay had to be still working, because the house was very quiet. He headed down a hallway. Two bedrooms were on the left and a third on the right, the door was partially closed. Removing his hat, he pushed it open and stepped inside.

A frail woman with white hair lay propped up in the bed, looking through a photo album. Oxygen tubing was fixed in her nose. Her beauty had long faded and her face was lined with smoker's wrinkles. This wasn't a seductress, a temptress. This was a dying woman. Chance wanted to say something but words failed him.

Blanche closed the album. "You look so much like your father." Her voice was raspy.

"You knew him well?"

"Oh, yes. He was madly in love with me. All men are."

Chance was taken aback at her boldness, and any sympathy for her vanished. "Why did you have to take him away from his family?"

"He was bored to death with that little mouse he was married to."

Chance crushed the rim of his hat in his hand, almost wanting to hit the woman.

"My mother was a beautiful, loving, caring person—someone you could never be."

"Oh, please. Her three-meals-a-day, clean-the-house type personality bored Chuck to death. He craved excitement, and that's what I gave him."

"Mom!" Shay stood in the doorway.

Chance saw the shock and the sadness in her green eyes. In that instant he knew that she knew. She'd known all along that her mother had been his father's mistress. And she hadn't told him. She hadn't said a word, just kept leading him on, letting him think they had a future. His heart stopped and it took a moment before he could catch his breath, a moment before he could accept that what he thought was real was as fake as the woman lying in the bed.

"Oh, Shay," Blanche said. "Mr. Hardin has come for a visit."

"Chance, please, could I talk to you outside?" Shay begged.

"No." He shook his head. "You had plenty of time to talk to me before now. I want the truth and your mother has no qualms about speaking her mind."

"Chance…"

He turned back to Blanche. "My dad wasn't rich. What was it about him that made you take him away from his family?"

"He lived in High Cotton," she said simply.

"Excuse me?" Chance's voice rose in astonishment.

"You want the truth, Mr. Hardin? I'll tell

you the truth. I love Jack. I've always loved him, and your father was my ticket back to High Cotton, back to Jack."

"I don't understand."

"Once Chuck got rid of his frumpy wife we could be together—in High Cotton."

"But Dad put money down on a house in Houston."

"That was your father's idea, not mine. I could make Chuck do anything. My plan was to live in High Cotton, where Jack could see me on another man's arm. He'd see me again and want me like always. Before long I'd be back at Southern Cross and Renee would be a thing of the past."

"What about my father?"

"He'd probably go back to his wife. I really didn't care."

Chance stepped closer to the bed. He had a death grip on his hat. "You must not have read the Jack Calhoun handbook very well."

The wrinkles on her face deepened. "What are you talking about?"

"Jack Calhoun was not a forgiving man. Once you cross him, you've sealed your fate. He took Renee back because he loved her, and he found out the supposed affair she was having was all lies—made up by you."

"Jack loved me."

"Whatever he felt for you was doomed the day you slept with another man. If you had stepped one foot back in High Cotton, Jack would have had you killed and your body would have never been found. And my dad's life would have been over, too. No one crosses Jack Calhoun."

"You're lying," Blanche insisted.

"You know that I'm not. When Harland brought you a message from Jack in that diner in Giddings, you knew he was telling the truth—either leave of your own free will or leave in a coffin. What was your response? You were on the first bus out of Giddings."

"Jack was just mad."

"Jack was dead serious and you knew it. That's why you got on that bus." Chance drew a harsh breath. "You used my father for nothing. For some insane, diabolical plan that makes no sense. You're the most evil person I've ever met. You killed my parents just as if you had taken a gun and shot them."

"Now wait a minute." Blanche's eyes almost bulged out of her head. "Shay, are you going to let him talk to me like that?"

"Yes," she replied.

"Get out!" Blanche screamed.

"Gladly." Chance left the room, holding on to what patience he had left.

"Chance." Shay caught him at the front door. "Please."

"No." He held up a hand. "Don't do that. Don't try to entice me with your eyes, your smile or your body. It's not going to work this time."

"I've never enticed you."

"Oh, please. Blanche Dumont is your mother. You know every feminine trick in the book, so let's end it now while I still have some pride left. Don't try to see me or contact me. Whatever we had is over."

He walked out, leaving behind everything he'd thought he wanted, everything he'd thought was real and perfect, only to find out he was being used just like his father.

Chapter Seventeen

Shay wasn't letting him get away with that. She followed him to the truck. "How dare you say that to me. You were the one pressuring me from the start. I told you I couldn't get involved, that it was complicated, but you kept on."

"It doesn't matter anymore, Shay," he said, his hand holding the open door.

"It matters when you accuse me of something I didn't do. And don't you *ever* imply that I'm like my mother."

"Why didn't you tell me?" he asked in a voice that twisted her stomach. "Why couldn't you have been honest with me?"

"How was I supposed to tell you something like that? It never seemed an appropriate time. I tried to tell you last night, but you wouldn't let me. I planned to tell you tonight."

"That's a little late, don't you think?"

"Yes," she admitted. "I'm a coward. I just couldn't cause you that much pain—pain like you're feeling now."

"Did you ever see my father?" he asked out of the blue.

"Yes. He came here many times. I was about five and I vaguely remember him. He talked about his three sons, and I wondered why he never brought them to play with me. The mind of a five-year-old."

"Hmm."

"If I could go back and change things, I'm not sure I would."

He frowned.

"I would have never gotten to know you and the wonderful man that you are." She stepped away from the truck. "So hate me if you must, if it eases your pain."

He looked into her eyes and she felt his agony like a physical blow. "It doesn't," he said.

"Nothing will ever change the way I feel about you. Nothing. I will always love you."

She turned and ran into the house. As she slammed the door she heard tires screeching on the pavement. Chance was gone and this time he really wasn't coming back. When he looked at her, all he could see was what her mother had done to his father. There was no way around that. No way to change the past. They'd been doomed from the start. Tears ran down her face. The ending was just too hard to bear.

"Mommy. Mommy," Darcy called, rushing into the house.

Shay wasn't ready to explain the situation to her daughter. But she wouldn't lie to Darcy, either.

"I saw Chance's truck. He didn't say hi."

Shay tried very hard to hide the tears on her face. She failed.

"Mommy, you're crying. Why are you crying?"

Shay sank to the floor because her knees could no longer hold her. Darcy curled up in her lap and Shay held her tightly.

"Why are you crying?" Darcy asked again.

She swallowed the lump in her throat. "Chance and I had an argument and he left."

"What about?"

Shay closed her eyes, fighting the urge to

lie. But she wouldn't do that this time. She had to tell Darcy the truth. "I did a bad thing. I kept something from Chance and I shouldn't have. You know what an honest and loyal man he is."

"Um-hmm."

"Sweetie." Shay brushed back Darcy's hair. "Chance won't be coming anymore. It's just you and me again."

Darcy looked up at her, her glasses askew. "But he loves us."

Shay's throat closed up and she fought back the tears.

"And Chance says you have to forgive. That's what he told me about the Bennett boys. So don't cry, Mommy."

Oh God. She prayed for help to handle this.

She straightened Darcy's glasses. "Go back to Nettie's. I just need some time alone."

"But…"

"No buts. Please mind me."

"Okay." Darcy picked up Tiny, who was whining at them, and slowly walked toward the kitchen.

Shay pushed herself to her feet and made her way to Blanche's room. After stepping inside, she slammed the door so hard the pictures on the walls shook.

"How could you be so cruel?"

"I told you to get rid of him. I told you this was going to happen."

"And you made sure it did by being as vindictive as possible." Shay heaved a sigh. "And that insane plan. Did you really believe that it would work? That Jack Calhoun would magically be back in your life?"

Blanche pointed a finger at her. "It would have worked if that stupid Chuck hadn't screwed it up. He screwed up my life, so what do I care if his kid gets his feelings hurt."

Shay tried to maintain her composure. "What about me? My feelings?"

Blanche looked confused.

"I love him, and to see him hurt like this is tearing me apart. You just had to make his pain worse and for that I will never forgive you. I've always been there for you, but you've never been there for me. When they found the first tumor, I held you while you cried. When you went through chemo and your hair fell out, I fitted you for a wig and told you that you were still beautiful. When the tumors came back and the doctors said they were inoperable, I was there for you every step of the way. I put my life on hold to care for you."

"I'm your mother."

Shay gave a sarcastic laugh. "Now there's a mouthful. You don't even know the meaning of the word."

"Shay, I'm getting tired of your little hissy fit."

"You know what I'm tired of, Blanche?"

Blanche stared at her with dull eyes.

"I'm tired of caring for an ungrateful, unfeeling excuse for a mother."

"Shay!" Blanche was shocked and reasonably so. Shay had never spoken to her or anyone else like that before, but anger was driving her on.

"Take a good look around, Mom. This may be the last night you spend in this room."

"What?"

"I should have put you in a nursing home from the start, like Nettie suggested, but oh no, I had to do the right thing. Prepare yourself, Blanche, because you're going into one now."

"This is my house."

"After I paid off all the debts you had against it, the house became mine. It's in my name."

"Shay, you can't do this. I'm your mother."

"That never counted for anything before

and it doesn't now." She turned on her heel and left.

In her room she fell across the bed and let the tears flow. She cried for herself and Darcy, and for the empty days and nights that were to come. She cried for a love that had gotten mangled by the past. But most of all she cried for Chance and the pain she'd caused him.

She felt the bed move and then two little arms went around her neck. "Don't cry, Mommy. Chance will be back."

She held her daughter with all the love she had in her. Darcy gave her the strength to face the next day, and the next. She would survive, but life would never be the same again.

Chance sat in his living room, staring into space, and all he could hear was *I will always love you.* It was about so much more. Couldn't she see that? It was about trust and faith. If she had trusted him, had faith in their love, then… Who was he kidding? Her mother had destroyed his parents' lives, and his, and Cadde's and Kid's. There was no way around that. Not even love could surmount that obstacle.

The door opened and Cadde and Kid walked in.

"How did it go?" Kid asked, plopping down onto the sofa.

"She knew. She's known all along," he replied in a voice he didn't recognize.

"I tried to tell you."

"Shut up," Cadde said, and sat by Kid. "How are you?"

"I feel as if I'm floating in outer space with a knife stuck in my heart," Chance answered. And then he told them the rest of the story. He wasn't keeping any more secrets.

"Son of a bitch." Kid jumped to his feet. "That's pure insanity."

"She didn't care anything about Dad. He was just a means to an end—getting back to Jack Calhoun."

"And he would have sliced and diced her up like goose liver," Cadde said.

"Yeah, but she just won't let herself believe that. In her demented mind she believes that she was the love of Jack's life. That's why she wanted those stupid rings back, and I even encouraged Renee to return them. I wish now that I had encouraged her to stuff them down Blanche's throat."

"Come on, little brother, bitterness doesn't become you," Kid remarked.

"You know," Cadde mused, "I was just a kid, but I vaguely remember her. She was a cross between Marilyn Monroe and Pamela Anderson—a real bombshell sex kitten. Jack bought her a red convertible Cadillac specially made for her. Funny how I remember that."

"You should see her now," Chance said. "She's a cross between the bad witch in *The Wizard of Oz,* and *Dracula.*"

"Damn. I need a drink." Kid headed for the liquor cabinet. "Oh, man, here's some Kentucky bourbon. How about a shot?"

"Pour away," Cadde said, and Chance nodded.

Kid handed them each a shot glass and held his up. "Here's to gorgeous women who make our lives hell. And, Blanche Dumont, may God have mercy on your scheming soul."

They downed the liquor and Kid poured another round.

"I'm not getting drunk," Chance stated. "My mind's messed up enough."

"Do you have anything better to do?" Kid lifted an eyebrow.

"No." Chance took the glass.

Kid raised his one more time. "Here's to the future and Shilah Oil. Under the Hardin boys' guidance may it prosper for a very long time."

"Hear, hear!" Cadde toasted and downed another shot, as did Chance and Kid.

Chance placed his glass carefully on the table. "I keep wondering if Blanche could have gotten Dad to live in High Cotton and flaunt their affair in front of Mom. Blanche said she could make him do anything."

Cadde twisted the glass in his hand. "But I'm betting she couldn't make him do that. That's why he was planning to buy a house." Cadde paused. "I just can't make myself believe that he would do that to Mom, his first love, his high school sweetheart."

"Me, neither," Kid said, resuming his seat. "And since we'll never know, we get to make the call." He placed his glass beside Chance's. "Now, boys, let's put the past where it belongs—in the past, and get busy running Shilah Oil."

"Damn, Kid, you took the words right out of my mouth." Cadde stood. "But it might be a little harder for Chance."

Chance ran his hands over his face. "It'll take time."

His brothers exchanged glances, but he ignored their worried looks.

His cell buzzed and he reached for it on his belt. In a moment he clicked off. "The Crocker well is back in business. They're drilling as I speak."

"Hot damn. That's the kind of news I like to hear." Cadde slapped Kid on the back.

"Get those gigantic paws off me." Kid shrugged away.

Life was back to normal, or as normal as it could be. Cadde and Kid would move on. Since they weren't at the scene and hadn't heard their parents talking, they weren't as emotionally affected as Chance. He had to find the strength to move on without the life he'd planned.

Without Shay.

As Cadde and Kid bickered back and forth, Chance heard her voice. *I will always love you.*

The days that followed were difficult for Shay. That first night Blanche called and called for her, but she stoically refused to answer. At midnight, Darcy shook her.

"Mommy, Blanche is calling you."

Shay knew she couldn't keep this up. It was

affecting Darcy. She crawled out of bed and went to see what her mother wanted.

"Do you need something?"

"Shay, please…"

"I'm not putting you in a home. Is that what you want to hear?" Shay had said it out of spite and anger, but she couldn't go through with it. The mother-daughter thing was hell sometimes.

"Could I have a glass of water?" Blanche asked, and Shay had never heard that note of entreaty in her voice before.

Shay got the water and set it on the nightstand. "Please get some sleep. It's late."

"I need my pills."

She felt a moment of remorse. Blanche needed her medication to rest. Shay opened the drawer and fished out the bottle. Handing it to her mother, she said, "Now maybe you can relax."

"Yes."

"Talk to you in the morning." Shay walked across the hall and fell into bed. Darcy sneaked in beside her.

"Can I sleep with you, Mommy?"

Shay pulled her close. Darcy was confused by the events of the day, and Shay wanted her to feel secure. Clutching her in her arms, Tiny at the foot of the bed, she went to sleep with visions of a dark-eyed Texan dancing in her head.

Chance threw himself into the oil business with a fervor. Many days he worked alongside the roughnecks, pulling pipe, keeping the drilling bit cool by pumping mud and water into the hole. He worked the pulleys, the hydraulic lift, the winch, and kept the generators going. By the end of the day he was covered in mud, oil and grime, but he welcomed the physical labor. It was what he needed to hold the memories at bay. When he fell into bed, though, it didn't keep him from seeing her green eyes.

He opened the apartment door at 8:00 p.m., dog tired. Quickly stripping off his filthy clothes, he took a shower. He slipped on Jockey shorts and headed for the living room and the hamburgers he'd picked up. When he went into restaurants dirty from the oil fields, people tended to frown at him. So he usually hopped into his truck and took the drive-through route.

As he finished devouring one burger and started another, his cell buzzed. He dashed to the bedroom to answer it. His hand paused when he saw the caller ID: Shay Dumont.

Why was she phoning? He'd told her not to. Hearing her voice would just be too hard to take. He'd let it ring. Then, of its own violation, his hand reached for it. He couldn't seem to stop himself.

"Chance, this is Darcy." At the sound of her voice he realized how much he missed that kid.

He let out a sigh of relief. "Hey, hotshot."

"Are you okay?"

"I'm fine." He paused, wondering if Shay had put her up to calling. "How did you get my number?"

"I saw it on a piece of paper in Mommy's purse when I was looking for gum. She doesn't know I called, so I have to talk real low."

"What's up?"

"Mommy's really sad."

"Oh." *Darcy, don't do this to me.* He didn't want to hear anything about Shay.

"Mommy said she kept something from you and it made you angry. But she would never hurt anyone. She's the best person ever. I know she's sorry, so now you can forgive her."

"Darcy, it's not that simple."

"Yes, it is. When the Bennett boys busted

my lip you said I had to forgive because that's what a good person does. So I did. You're a good person. Why can't you forgive Mommy?"

"Darcy…"

"If you can't forgive Mommy, then I don't want you for a daddy anymore."

The phone went dead and he stared at it as if it was about to explode. *You have to forgive.* Now he had to eat those words.

It hit him like a two-by-four right between the eyes. His father had done the same thing. He had spouted words about fidelity to his sons and how important it was to a marriage. Then Blanche Dumont had entered his life and all rational thought had left his mind. Everything he'd taught his sons had flown out the window.

Just as everything Chance had taught Darcy seemed to be for someone else—not him. Was he more like his father than he'd ever imagined?

As Chance reached the living room, Kid walked in. Chance frowned at him.

"Okay. I forgot to knock," he said with a sheepish grin. Looking around, he asked, "You have someone here?"

"No. Why?" Chance sat on the sofa and placed his phone by his burger.

Kid waved a hand toward him. "You're in your underwear."

"So? I'm in my home. I can be naked if I want to."

"That's good, too." Kid reached over, picked up the half-eaten burger and took a bite.

"Hey, that's my supper."

"You bought two. I know you did 'cause you always do." Kid sank into the comfy chair, still eating the burger.

"That doesn't give you the right to eat it," Chance said on his way to the refrigerator for milk.

"Come on, Chance. I'm hungry."

"They will sell you food, Kid. You do know that, right?" He resumed his seat, sipping a glass of milk.

"Smart-ass." Kid finished the burger and wiped his hands on his jeans. "I have a dinner and dancing date later with Molly."

"It's already nine o'clock," Chance reminded him, staring at his cell phone. *You have to forgive Mommy. A good person does that. You said so.*

"Some people do have a social life." Kid watched him. "Why do you keep staring at your cell as if it's about to sprout wings and fly?"

Chance placed the half-full glass by his phone. "Darcy called."

"Shay's daughter?"

"Yes."

"What did she want?"

"To teach me a lesson."

"What?"

Chance told him about the Bennett boys.

"So you encouraged her to forgive?"

"I did, and I believe everything I told her. But I have a hard time practicing what I preached." He rubbed the back of his neck. "I can't help but wonder if Dad felt the same way."

"Probably," Kid admitted. "He was a man and he had weaknesses, as we now know. But who knows what we, his sons, are going to do in the future. Sometimes we're shaped by the people around us."

Chance stared at his brother. "Did you just say that?"

Kid looked around. "I think. Has to be the most profound thing I've ever said."

"I'll say."

Kid leaned forward, his elbows on his

knees. "Listen, Chance, I don't know a lot about women but—"

"If you don't, then who does?"

"I'm serious here."

"Sometimes it's hard to tell."

"I am, so listen. It's not often I impart knowledge."

Chance refrained from laughing.

"Shay is not Blanche, just like you, me and Cadde are not Dad. I think you have that a little mixed up in your hard head. If the love you have for Shay is the twenty-four-carat-gold, slip-on-the-left-hand kind, you better think twice before throwing it away. If it's the real deal, you'll see her face in every woman you date. She'll always be there at the back of your mind. You'll remember little things about her that used to drive you crazy—her smile, her humor…"

"Are we talking about you or me?"

"We're talking about you, damn it. I've never been in love."

"What about Lucky?"

"That was puppy love, for crying out loud, Chance. Pay attention."

"I heard every word, Kid, and I'll heed your advice."

"Good." He stood. "It's not often I give advice to the lovelorn." He reached down and picked up the glass of milk and drained it.

"Hey."

Kid ignored his objection, as usual. "I have a date, so I have to run. Listen to Darcy. She's smarter than you are. And get that hangdog look off your face and do something about your life instead of working yourself to death." He strolled to the door.

"Kid?"

Kid glanced back.

"Thanks."

"Anytime, little brother."

As the door closed, Chance went back to the kitchen for more milk. Was their love the twenty-four-carat-gold, slip-on-the-left-hand kind? He had thought so. What had changed? *Shay is not Blanche.* Kid was right. He did have that connection confused in his mind. Shay was nothing like her mother.

You have to forgive Mommy.

Could he do that?

Could he truly put the past behind him?

Only time would tell.

Chapter Eighteen

With each day, Blanche grew worse, and finally hospice was called in. The doctor had ordered a morphine drip to keep the pain at bay. Her breathing was shallow and difficult. Shay knew her mother would not be with her much longer. As much as she had prepared herself, it still wasn't easy.

If she even left the room, Blanche became agitated. Shay had to stop working to care for her, and had to drop out of summer class at the university. Quitting work was a big decision, because now they would have no income. She had a little nest egg tucked away and they had to live on that. Somehow they would survive.

It was early August and Darcy wasn't back in school yet, which was a good thing. Shay's main focus had to be on her mother.

One night Blanche's coughing woke her. She got up from the chair and could see she was in distress. Picking up the phone, she dialed 911. The ambulance arrived in minutes and whisked Blanche away to the hospital.

Shay ran into Darcy's room and gathered her and Tiny into her arms, then ran next door. It was one o'clock in the morning, so it took Nettie a while to get to the door.

Last week there had been a robbery down the street, and Shay knew Nettie was being cautious. She pounded on the door with her fist. "Nettie, it's me. Open up."

The door opened a crack and the older woman, her gray hair askew, peered out. Undoing the chain, she said, "Come in, child."

Shay handed over her load. Darcy didn't even stir. "The ambulance just picked up Blanche. I have to go. Please take care of Darcy."

"Of course."

She kissed Nettie's wrinkled cheek. "I don't know what I'd do without you."

"You'll never have to find out, child, because I'm always here for you. You know that."

"Thank you." With that, Shay was off, running through the dark. She remembered so many times she'd made this same trek as a kid, afraid the darkness was going to eat her up.

She held out her arms. "Come and get me," she said to the night. She could handle anything. She'd been tempered by the fire of rejection, the evil of bitterness and the cruelties of life. All that was left was the dying.

Could she handle that—alone?

Within minutes she was in her car and headed for the hospital. The E.R. people were trying to get Blanche stabilized. Shay waited in a small room.

Finally, the doctor came out. He handed her a small envelope. "Your mother's rings are enclosed. Valuables should be kept at home. They can so easily be stolen."

"Thank you," she said, taking the envelope. What should she do with them?

"Ms. Dumont, I'm afraid it's not going to be much longer. Would you like me to call someone so you won't be alone?"

But she was alone. The person she wanted to be here would never come. Though she needed him more than she'd ever needed anyone.

"No. Thank you."

The doctor nodded. "We're moving her to ICU. You can sit with her there."

"Thank you."

Shay put the rings in her purse and made her way upstairs. Her hair was everywhere, like Nettie's. She fished for a clip in her purse, but couldn't find one, so gave up. The nurse showed her to Blanche's cubicle. The unit was round, so the nurses at the station had a clear view of every patient.

Shay sat by her mother's bedside. Blanche was so pale, so still. When she turned her head, Shay almost jumped out of her chair. Her mother weakly opened her eyes.

"Ci-ga-rette." The word came out low, but Shay heard it.

"Mom, you can't have a cigarette. You haven't had one in over four years and you certainly can't have one in here."

"J-just…hold."

How was she supposed to find a cigarette in a hospital? But being the dutiful daughter, she went in search of one. She stopped at the nurses' station.

"Does anyone have a cigarette?"

Four pairs of eyes stared at her in disbelief.

"Oh, no, it's not for me," she hastened to

say. "I don't smoke. My mother just wants to hold one."

They glanced at each other and shook their heads. No one smoked.

"Thanks." She made her way back to her mother's bedside. Before she could sit down, a nurse who'd been at the station tucked a cigarette into her hand and walked away.

Evidently, she didn't want anyone to know she smoked, and rightfully so. She'd probably get a daily lecture. The woman worked in a hospital and saw death on a regular basis—a lot of it caused by smoking. Shay didn't quite get that. But it was her choice, her decision. Shay had her own problems.

She placed the cigarette between her mother's forefinger and middle one. "Mom?" she murmured.

Blanche opened her eyes and saw the cigarette. She managed a faint smile. "You're... a...good...daughter."

"Please don't try to talk," Shay begged, as her mother struggled to breathe. But she soaked up the words like dry cotton.

"I'm...sorry."

And just like that, the years of resentment and bitterness disappeared. Her mother had never said she was sorry, so Shay knew she meant it. And for her own peace of mind, Shay took it to mean she was sorry for hurting Chance.

"Love...you," Blanche whispered, and raised her hand to sniff the cigarette. "Ah..." Suddenly the cigarette fell to the bed, and Blanche gasped for air. Her chest rose and slowly relaxed, and Shay knew her mother had gone to a happier place. The monitors attached to Blanche went off like a fire alarm. Two nurses came running in and Shay moved away as they checked her over.

One nurse looked at Shay. "I'm sorry. She's passed on."

"I know," Shay replied, and took her mother's limp hand. "I love you, too." She walked out and down the hall to a waiting room, and collapsed in a chair. She was mentally and physically drained. The waiting area was empty, and that's the way she felt inside— empty and alone.

Shay had thought that she was prepared, but as tears rolled down her cheeks she realized she wasn't. The mother-daughter bond had been bent, bruised and almost severed, but it was still there to the bitter end. So many lies and deceit, and yet their relationship had survived in its own unique way.

Shay chewed on a nail, then forced herself to stop. While Chance had been in her life, she'd been happy and had stopped biting her nails. Now…

Her mother had hurt so many people. Shay would never understand that, but she sincerely hoped Blanche was now at peace. More tears rolled from her eyes and she wrapped her arms around her waist to stop the trembling.

She needed two strong arms to hold her, to console her. But Chance was never going to forgive her, and now she had to live with the consequences of her actions.

To live without Chance.

Chance was in his office, typing notes and comments into the computer so Cadde could see the progress, or lack of progress, on each site. The tool pushers sent notes in, too, so Cadde had a clear picture on the status of the wells.

Chance paused over the Crocker well notes. The pumpjack had been set two weeks ago and the well was producing over two hundred barrels a day. Cadde would probably dance on his desk at these figures. It was good for the Crocker family and for Shilah Oil.

Kid marched in and slapped a newspaper

in front of Chance. It was turned to the obit-
uaries.

"Blanche Dumont died," he said.

"So?"

Kid stuck the paper in his face.

Chance stared at the picture of Blanche
in her younger days, when she could turn a
man's head. His gut tightened, but he looked
at the woman. For the first time he admitted
that Shay resembled her mother only slightly.
They had the same blonde hair and green
eyes, but the shape of the face and eyes were
different. Their personalities were different,
too. Shay was caring, loving and good all the
way to her soul. As Darcy had said, her mom
would never hurt anyone.

He let out a long breath.

Shay is not Blanche.

Funny how looking at a picture had brought
the truth to the surface—a truth that had been
temporarily hiding beneath the pain. He drew
another breath and let the pain ebb from his
system.

He wasn't his father, either. He was his own
person and had his own mistakes to make. He
briefly read the obit and wondered how Shay
was doing. How was she coping?

Kid leaned over and placed both hands flat

on the desk, his face inches from Chance's. "What you do now will determine your future. Make sure you do the right thing."

"Are you reading some sort of book on wisdom?" Chance asked, his voice teasing.

"Hell, no. The wisdom I have I got from Aunt Etta."

"But who knew you were listening?"

The conversation was interrupted by Cadde. "Chance, do you have the figures on the Crocker well?"

"I just sent them to your computer."

"Good."

Kid pointed to the paper. "Blanche Dumont died."

"Oh." Cadde glanced at Chance. "Are you okay?"

"Yep. I'm going to be fine." He leaned back in his chair. "Blanche destroyed our parents' lives for some selfish reason of her own. I can't change that and I can't keep holding all this anger inside me. They were adults and made their own choices. Now I have to make mine."

Cadde nodded. "Sounds as if you've come to grips with it."

"Yep." He leaned forward. "It's time to move on."

"Wise advice." Cadde turned to Kid. "Did you read the geologist and engineer report on our leases in the Eagle Ford area?"

"Yes. They're damn good and should be very productive for Shilah Oil. We just have to get Jessie to agree."

"I can handle Jessie."

"Since when?" Kid asked as they walked out. "You haven't made any progress in that direction in months. Hell, I have a better chance of persuading her than you do."

"Shut up, Kid, and go to work."

They bickered all the way down the hall, and Chance smiled for the first time in weeks. He was going to be okay. His brothers had his back and the world looked brighter than usual.

He stood and stared out the window, wondering if he and Shay could find their way back to each other.

Would the past always be an obstacle?

The day of the funeral dawned cloudy and there was rain in the forecast. Shay thought it was fitting for a woman whose life had been fraught with heartache and pain.

There was only a graveside service, with her, Darcy and Nettie attending. Blanche had alienated her friends a long time ago. The pastor from Shay and Darcy's church performed a short ceremony and Darcy read a prayer. Just like that, a life ended.

Shay said a silent goodbye to a woman she didn't understand, a woman she barely knew—one who'd flittered in and out of her life from time to time. Blanche certainly wasn't a baking-cookies, PTA type mom, but could dish out guilt like cheesecake. She hadn't been a mother at all. With Nettie's help, Shay had practically raised herself. But the blood bond was there.

Now it was over. Shay prayed her mother had found some sort of peace.

Nettie nodded over her shoulder and Shay turned to see what she was nodding at.

A black Cadillac Escalade drove up to the curb. A tall, broad-shouldered man got out on the driver's side. Shay knew who he was from the pictures she'd seen at Southern Cross—Judd Calhoun. A black-haired, beautiful woman joined him—Caitlyn, his wife. From the backseat she saw Renee emerging. What were they doing here?

"Darcy, stay with Nettie," she said, and walked toward them.

When she reached Judd, he said, "I was

never too fond of Blanche, but my mother wanted to come today and I couldn't let her come alone."

Caitlyn hugged her. "I'm so sorry for your loss."

"Thank you," Shay replied, a little dazed.

Renee hugged her in a cloud of Chanel. "Sugar, I'm so sorry—so sorry for everything you had to go through."

"Th-thank you."

"I don't know why I didn't think of this when I brought you the rings." Renee reached into the car and pulled out a large velvet box.

Shay recognized it and took a step backward. "No," she muttered.

"This is Blanche's jewelry. You should have it," the woman insisted.

"No," she said again. "I could never take it. It's tainted with too much heartache and betrayal." She opened her purse and fished out the rings. "Take these, too. I don't want them. It was such a nice gesture, but I can't keep them."

"Oh, Shay," Renee murmured, and there was nothing but sincerity in her voice.

"How can you be so nice to me? My mother was your worst enemy. She hurt you, lied about you and destroyed your first marriage."

Renee touched her cheek. "Sugar, I'm not doing this for Blanche. I'm doing this for you."

"Oh." The response took the wind out of her lungs. Could they possibly see her as her own person and not Blanche's daughter?

"Tell you what I'll do," Judd said. "I'll have the jewelry appraised, sell it and send you the money."

"You can use it for your daughter's education," Caitlyn suggested. "Use it for good and forget about the bad stuff."

"I don't know what to say. I'm overwhelmed."

"That's understandable, sugar," Renee said.

It was starting to drizzle, and Judd glanced toward the sky.

"We better go. It looks as if a downpour is coming."

Shay waved with tears in her eyes as they drove away, and then she walked back to her daughter and Nettie. The Calhouns' presence here today was truly a gift. They had forgiven her. How she wished Chance could make the same effort.

They stood for a moment longer at the gravesite in the drizzling rain.

"I'm getting wet," Darcy said.

"Then let's go, child." Nettie took her hand.

Shay stared at the coffin and vowed that she would leave all the bad stuff here: the anger, the bitterness, the resentment and the evil schemes of her mother. From this day forward she would try to fill her and Darcy's lives with goodness.

Darcy screamed and Shay whirled around to see what she was upset about. Darcy was flying across the lawn to a man getting out of a big silver truck.

Chance!

Shay's heart knocked against her ribs so hard that she had to take a breath.

Darcy barreled into Chance, who lifted her and swung her around. She squealed with delight and wrapped her arms around his neck. A moment later she slid to the grass, took Chance's hand and led him toward Shay.

She didn't know she was holding her breath until the pain in her chest told her so. She gulped in air.

"See, Mommy? I told you Chance would come."

And he had. Now what did she say?

Darcy gave Nettie a thumbs-up and whispered, "The love potion worked."

"What?" Shay looked at Nettie, who was

frowning at the child. What had those two concocted? She decided to let it ride. She had more important things on her mind—like the man standing in front of her.

Nettie grabbed Darcy's hand. "Let's go to the car. We're getting wet."

Unlike her usual behavior, Darcy went meekly. That left Shay and Chance alone with a gulf of pain between them.

She watched the rain tap-tapping on the plastic cover on his Stetson. She wanted to look into his eyes, but was afraid of what she would see.

"How are you?" he asked in a deep, soothing voice, that gave her the courage to raise her eyes to his. She caught her breath at what she saw there. The fog of pain had cleared, replaced by a look of peace. Dare she hope…?

She swallowed and said what was in her heart. "I need someone to hold me."

He opened his arms and she flew into them, pressing against him. He held her in a viselike grip, his breath warm on her wet forehead.

"I'm sorry, Shay. I'm sorry."

"Shh." She pressed her fingers against his lips. "Please don't apologize. You have nothing to be sorry for."

"I just got lost in the past."

"And now?" she asked, staring up at him, tasting the rain on her lips.

"I want a life, a normal life, with a woman I love."

"Oh, Chance." She stood on tiptoes to meet his kiss, and gave herself up to him and to everything that was yet to come in their lives. "I love you," she whispered against his lips.

"I love you, too," he groaned. "And that's what was so hard about all this. Our love was being destroyed by our parents, and I couldn't seem to change that."

Shay buried her face against his damp shirt. "What changed your mind?"

"Darcy and Kid."

"What?" She raised her head.

"Darcy called and said that I had to forgive you. And then she reminded me what I'd told her about forgiveness. It's kind of eye-opening to have your words quoted back to you by an eight-year-old."

"I didn't even know she'd called." It seemed as if her daughter had been very busy lately. But for the life of her Shay couldn't find anything wrong with that. "And Kid? What did he say?"

Chance's arms tightened around her. "He

said if what I felt for you was the twenty-four-carat-gold, slip-on-the-left-hand kind, then I'd better hang on to it."

She looked up at him. "So do we have that kind of love?"

He smiled and her heart melted. "I'm willing to bet that we do."

"Me, too." She burrowed into him, feeling loved. She had finally found the real thing.

"Do you know that it's pouring down rain?" he asked with a note of humor in his voice.

"Yes. Does it matter?"

"No. I'll love peeling off your clothes later."

She looked through the rain at this incredible man who loved her, and said, "I love you. No matter what, I will always love you."

His lips caught hers in a fiery kiss that bonded them together forever. Later, they would talk about their parents, and would be armed with a love so strong it could hurdle the obstacles of the past. They weren't looking back. They were moving forward.

Epilogue

Six Months Later

Chance leaned on the white board fence, watching Darcy ride her new horse, Sparky. She was born to the saddle, as Uncle Rufus would say, already galloping around the corral like a pro.

So much had changed in the last six months. They'd been married in Shay's church, surrounded by family—Aunt Etta and Uncle Rufus were there, as well as the Calhouns and the Belles. Shay was a little overwhelmed by his extended family, but it didn't take her long to love them, too.

They'd searched for a house, but couldn't find one to suit them. Then Chance found a two-story colonial with barns and a pond, on twenty acres between Houston and Brenham. He thought it was perfect. Shay thought the house was too big, but the private bedroom and bath off the kitchen persuaded her. It would be Nettie's private space.

But Nettie had other ideas. Once Nettie and Shay put their old houses on the market, she surprised them by saying she'd found an assisted living facility that she liked, and had signed a contract. Shay was devastated, but nothing she said changed Nettie's mind.

Petey's parents got back together and they moved to Arlington. He and Darcy wrote each other and talked on the phone. Darcy didn't have time to be sad. She had a whole new life.

She galloped toward him now and pulled up, rubbing Sparky's neck. "I asked Mommy something and she said I had to ask you."

"What did you ask her?"

The girl took a long time petting her horse. Finally, she looked up and straightened her glasses. "I asked her if I could call you Daddy."

His heart knocked against his ribs. "Since

I'm adopting you, I think that would be nice." He swallowed. "I am your father now, Darcy."

"Cool," she said, and galloped away.

Chance didn't think it was possible to be any happier. He had everything he'd ever wanted—Shay, Darcy, a new home and a new life. They didn't talk much about their parents. They didn't need to. They had finally put the past to rest.

Judd, as promised, had mailed Shay a check for the jewelry, and they had put the money in trust for Darcy's education. At least some good had come out of the horrible affair.

"Mommy's coming," Darcy shouted, waving like crazy.

He turned to see the silver Tahoe he'd given her as a wedding gift roll into the garage.

Moments later, two slim arms circled him from behind. "Ah, this feels good."

With one arm, he reached around and pulled her in front of him. "Try it from this angle."

She giggled and pressed into him. "Much better," she cooed.

He kissed her gently, softly, and rested his forehead against hers. "How was school?" Shay was now going to college full time.

"Same ol', same ol'." She played with the buttons on his shirt. "I can't believe I graduate in three months."

He lifted her chin. "Then why the glum face?"

"I went by Nettie's."

"Oh."

"I was hoping to find her miserable so I could bring her home, but she was laughing and talking with a group, playing dominoes."

"So she's happy?"

"I suppose. She's telling fortunes, and the lady who does hair there quit, so she's now doing hair again until they can find someone else."

"Sounds as if she's found her niche."

"I know, but…"

"But what?"

"I would have never gotten through my awful childhood if it hadn't been for Nettie. I want to be there for her like she was for me."

He kissed the side of Shay's face. "Let Nettie have her independence. Further down the road I'm sure she'll need us, and we will be there for her."

"I know." Shay rested her head against him and he stroked her hair as his other hand crept beneath her knit top.

"Okay, mister, we're out here in broad daylight with our daughter watching."

He smiled and took her lips one more time.

"Watch me, Mommy," Darcy called, and galloped full speed around the corral.

Shay turned in the circle of Chance's arms. "Oh, isn't that too fast?"

"Pull her up, hotshot," he shouted.

"Okay, Daddy." Darcy yanked the reins a moment before she reached the fence, and dust blanketed them.

"Darcy," Shay scolded.

"Sorry, Mom."

Chance pointed a finger at her. "Not again, hotshot."

"Okay, Daddy." Then Darcy quickly changed the subject. "Are we going to High Five this weekend?"

"Yes, we are," he answered.

"Oh, boy. I get to play with Haley, Georgie, Val, Kira—and the twins." She rolled her eyes as she mentioned the toddlers.

"I thought you liked them," Shay said.

"I do, but they keep pulling my glasses off."

"I'm sure you can cope," Shay commented.

"Yeah." She nodded. "And I get to hold

the baby. I like babies." After delivering that news, she cantered away.

Dane Cooper Yates, heir apparent to High Five, had been born in July. He was growing by leaps and bounds.

Shay looked at Chance. "That was not very subtle. How do *you* feel about babies?"

"Anything you want." He felt a grin spread across his face.

"I'd like to wait until I finish my degree."

"Okay, but we'll practice a whole lot in the meantime."

She laughed and burrowed against him. "So we're going to High Five?"

"Yep, Uncle Rufus found a horse for you. Her name is Goldie. A golden horse for a golden lady."

She looked up at him, her eyes wistful. "I'm not my mother. I don't need material things. I just need you."

"Oh, honey." He held her tight and for a moment they were lost in a love that had survived against all odds.

She moved her head against him. "She's calling you Daddy."

"Yes, and it feels right."

Shay's arms encircled his neck and brought

his lips down to hers, and nothing was said for some time.

Chance had learned a hard lesson: forgiveness brought immeasurable rewards. And the greatest reward of all was Shay's love.

He would remember that for the rest of his life.

* * * * *